"I'm not plotting to entrap you."

Josey added, "The trouble with you, Thorne Macallan, is your ego. You automatically assume you can make any woman you meet your lover. But I am the exception. You don't appeal to me, and you never would."

"Tell Maud for me it worked," he said deliberately as he forced her chin up until she saw the bitter triumph in his eyes. "You're not the exception, as you boasted. Far from it. I want you, and I can take you anytime I like. But it will be when *I* choose, not at Maud's choosing or yours. When *I* decide, Josey Smith, I'll become your lover."

"I'll see you in hell first!" she snarled.

"Tell Maud that," he drawled, "so she'll remember the next time she's tempted to play God."

Books by Lillian Cheatham

LILLIAN CHEATHAM

lady with a past

Harlequin Books

TORONTO • NEW YORK • LONDON
AMSTERDAM • PARIS • SYDNEY • HAMBURG
STOCKHOLM • ATHENS • TOKYO • MILAN

Harlequin Presents first edition August 1985
ISBN 0-373-10808-7

Original hardcover edition published in 1985
by Mills & Boon Limited

Printed in U.S.A.

CHAPTER ONE

T. J. MACALLAN, counsellor-at-law, listened boredly as his fellow attorney presented his case, his hard, handsome face a mask behind which a cold, remorseless brain probed for flaws. His lids drooped lazily over a pair of keen, grey eyes as he lounged carelessly in his chair, long, lean fingers playing idly with a pencil on the table. He did not need to prove himself—at barely thirty, he was already one of the most brilliant young lawyers in the State.

He did not usually bother with a case this small, but he had accepted it because of an appeal from an old friend, who knew Tony Leyden's parents. His client was a young man who had had the misfortune to fall in love with the wrong woman. A cold smile touched his lips. The mercenary little bitch was going to share the guilt with him, and he was going to enjoy cutting her down to size.

Jocelyn watched him compulsively, noting the powerful shoulders, the lean, tapering thighs beneath the fine, wool suit. He was a man who would always stand out in a crowd. His looks were devastating, of course, but it was also a matter of sheer masculine grace and a self-assurance that came with power—raw, male power. She shivered in her cheap little dress. She was pinning all her hopes, her faith on him. Her own lawyer, from the Public Defender's office, was hopelessly incompetent. She was already regretting his advice to forego a jury trial and throw herself on the mercy of the court.

Then, Macallan started speaking and she listened in growing disbelief, stunned to realise that the greedy little opportunist he was portraying was herself. She dimly heard her lawyer's objections, the judge's overruling, but she heard every cruel distortion uttered in that cool, eloquent voice. She heard herself presented as a tease and Tony as a lovesick innocent; her moral principles twisted to sound like some deviant sex game she had played for money. When he finished, Jocelyn met the judge's eyes and she began to dimly comprehend what Macallan had done to her.

She was still dazed as she was being sentenced. She was given two years, the same as Tony, subject to parole after six months, and a stern, moralistic lecture by the judge on her past and future behaviour.

Then, she understood why Macallan had crucified her in public. By making her equally responsible for the stolen money, he had mitigated Tony's offence and gained a minimum sentence for him. She lost control then, bursting into impassioned speech and hurling insults at that cold, cruel face.

'You bastard!' she screamed. 'You lying, crooked, shyster bastard! I'll get you if it's the last thing I do! I'll make you pay for this day before I die! If I have to kill you, I'll make you pay!'

The next thing she knew, she was being dragged out of the courtroom, the judge pounding with his gavel. The last sight she had of T. J. Macallan maddened her. He was looking at her with a cold, remote distaste, as though she was a wild animal in a cage.

'So it was all a trick! A hoax played on me by you and Annie! And you don't regret a bit of it, do you?' Josey Smith eyed her friend with rueful severity.

They had been friends for six years—Josey, at twenty-five, was forty years younger than Maud Lorrimer. But that had made no difference in the quality of their friendship which, so far as Josey was concerned, was deathless. They had met at a low point in her life and Maud had, quite literally, saved her life. If she lived to be a hundred, she couldn't repay the debt but at the moment, she was tempted to murder her.

'Not at all,' Maud replied to her question smugly. 'It got you here, didn't it?'

Indeed, it had. All it had taken was Annie's emergency call telling her that Miss Maud had been taken to the hospital with a heart attack. After that, had come a long, agonising wait while Josey tried to get through to someone who could tell her something, then Maud, surprisingly, had been able to talk to her. She had reassured her that she was much better, but Thorne was insisting that she quit work and retire to a nursing home. Maud's work was her life—Josey knew that and thought Thorne should have known it. So she had promised as soon as she could get her own affairs in orders, she would be on the first plane out of Atlanta for Hilton Head.

All the way, she sizzled with fury at Thorne, Maud's nephew. How dare he threaten to put Maud, *her* Maud, of all people, in a nursing home! Maud, the liveliest kid on the block, the life of every party, the young at heart, in a horrible place like that! It had been so monstrous that she had arrived fighting mad. It rather took the wind out of her sails, therefore, to find Maud, not at death's door as she had been led to believe, but out on the terrace, a martini at her elbow. If Josey hadn't been so relieved, she would have been furious.

'They only kept me overnight for observation,' Maud breezily explained her hospital visit.

'And I suppose Thorne didn't really say anything about a nursing home, did he?' Josey asked sarcastically.

Maud grinned, her eyes as bright as a monkey's. 'Ask him yourself—he'll be here this weekend. Simmer down, love, take a load off your feet and have a drink. If I hadn't speeded up the process, you'd still be in Atlanta, cataloguing John's books for his lawyer. Lord, I'm going to miss old John!' she added wistfully.

Josey sighed, kicked off her shoes and sank into one of the comfortable redwood chairs that had been rolled forward to get the benefit of the pale November sunlight.

'So am I,' she said simply. 'That's why I got so upright when I thought you'd had a heart attack. His was so sudden. He worked that last day, you know, dictating the final chapters. His publisher is looking for someone to finish it.'

'You could have done it.'

'No, I'm not a historian.' She smiled affectionately at Maud. 'I may have bluffed John but I don't think my claim would hold up with his publisher.'

She ran her hands through her hair, loosening the prim knot at the back. Unrestrained, it tumbled to her shoulders, gleaming with copper highlights. Her face, untouched by make-up, raised itself gratefully to the sun. Not for the first time, Maud marvelled at Josey's beauty. Every feature of her face was sheer perfection: her cheekbones, nose, the soft mouth, those tawny eyes beneath slanting brows, with their extraordinary range of colour. Inside the dowdy clothes and flat, 'sensible' shoes, was a superb figure, its slender lines not immediately obvious to anyone but a connoisseur of women. Maud had wondered more than once at the traumatic experience that had turned this beautiful girl into a repressed woman. She made a sudden decision.

'I'm taking you shopping tomorrow and *I* choose the clothes,' she said abruptly.

Josey looked amused. 'You've made a rapid recovery,' she said drily.

Maud didn't bother to answer that. 'Well? No outcries of horror? No adamant refusal to allow me to spend a cent on you?'

'No need,' Josey said placidly. 'I have my own money now. I can buy my own clothes this time.'

'Ah, yes, the money John left you. Fifty thousand, wasn't it? I'm glad you're going to put it to good use.'

Josey flushed slightly. 'I'm only keeping a thousand for myself,' she replied defensively. 'I set up an annuity for old Maggie. She had worked for John for forty-five years, and she was destitute.'

'That would have pleased John,' Maud said slowly. 'Although he wanted you to have that money. He felt you deserved it. What did his cousins have to say about it?'

'Quite a lot.' Josey grimaced. 'They accused me of being John's mistress, among other things.

John, of all people! Why, he was like a father to me! And they begrudged Maggie getting a cent after all those years of faithful service.'

'Harpies!' Maud said angrily. 'They got the house. What more did they want?'

'All of it. But let's not talk about them.' Josey shivered, remembering the two avid old women at John's funeral, then later, picking their way through the house as they priced every piece of bric-à-brac in sight. 'Do you really want me to work for you, Maud? Are you sure you aren't inventing a job, just because I'm out of work?'

'Of course not. I need you.'

'And Thorne? What does he think about you hiring me?'

'Thorne?' Maud asked innocently. 'Since when have I ever allowed Thorne to tell me how to run my business?'

'Ever since I've known you,' Josey pointed out mildly. 'In spite of his never having done a day's work himself, he seems to have a good bit to say about your affairs. I know he bought this land and had this house built for you, and he took out the lease on your apartment in Atlanta, and you consult him every time you make a business move. The only thing I don't understand is why?'

Maud's eyes twinkled behind discreetly lowered lids. 'You see, my dear, he is a man.'

This provoked the reaction she expected. 'Maud Lorrimer, are you some kind of chauvinist? A man, indeed! That doesn't automatically make him a god! And from what I've heard of your nephew, he's something less than that! Information, incidentally, which you've given me yourself.'

'I?' Maud looked puzzled. 'Just because I've

mentioned that Thorne has an occasional problem
with the women in his life . . .'

'Occasional! He's a womaniser and you know
it!'

'He did rather tend, in his younger days, to
burn the candle at both ends . . .'

'Hah!'

'Josey, my dear, you must learn to curb your
prejudice,' Maud said reprovingly. 'My nephew
is a perfect gentleman and a reliable business
man. He'll be spending Christmas with us, and I
do want you to become friends. How can you
when you have such wicked thoughts about him?
Besides, don't you think it's wrong to pass
judgment on someone whom you've never met?
How can you know the real Thorne when you've
consistently refused to meet him?'

Josey gasped. 'Pardon me if I'm wrong, Maud,
but I distinctly remember you advising me that I
should avoid him because he wasn't to be
trusted.'

'*I*? Ridiculous!' Maud rose. 'Now, come along
and let's unpack your things. I want to see just
what the damage is before I take you shopping
tomorrow. And, Josey, dear, those shoes will
simply have to go.'

Josey trailed behind her bewilderedly. It must
be jet lag, she decided, although the brief ride
from Atlanta to Savannah, then the thirty minute
drive to this island off the coast of South Carolina
would not account for Maud's memory loss.
Obviously, Thorne was now in favour, although
Josey happened to remember he had once been a
source of great worry to his aunt. So far as
meeting him, Josey had cleared a wide swath
whenever that possibility came up. Maud's

warnings hadn't been the cause: it had been Josey's own antipathy towards his type of man.

She supposed she did tend to be prejudiced against Thorne, to despise him without really knowing him, Josey admitted reluctantly. After this, she would try to give him the benefit of the doubt, but she did hope he would take his usual skiing vacation at Christmas time. Perhaps he'd forget his promise—from what she knew of him, it was possible. Anything could happen by then.

Josey did not intend to work for Maud: she had been tricked into it. For one thing, Maud had a tendency to take over one's life if given the opportunity. She was a tireless matchmaker and always had some eligible man for Josey to meet. Some macho type, usually, with super good looks and an oversized ego. Like the mental picture Josey had of Thorne Lorrimer. Given her own way, Josey would have stayed on in Atlanta and looked for work, if Maud hadn't sent that cry for help. Which is exactly why she did it, of course.

On the way upstairs, Josey got a quick look at the house. There was a superb view of the ocean from the terrace and the architecture was suited to a beach house, with plenty of skylights and windows. Dark, heart-of-pine floors contrasted with pure white walls and black-beamed ceilings. In the living room, a starkly modern fireplace with a copper hood was open to both it and the dining room. Maud's decorator had done his work well, too, blending some of her treasured heirlooms with the best of modern furnishings.

Upstairs, Annie had left the windows of Josey's room open, and she saw with delight that they overlooked the ocean. A breeze was blowing in, rustling the drapes and the ruffled bed coverlet. Josey took a deep breath. She could be happy here, she knew. She loved the beach. It was a hold over from her childhood when her parents had taken her on vacations to the Gulf coast. The sand was pure white and the sea blue—nothing like the rowdy Atlantic. They had always rented the same cottage, with a swing and rocking chairs on the porch. At night, she and her father would walk to the pier for ice cream and she would watch the boys and girls dancing barefoot in the sand to the blare of the jukebox.

She had loved those long, lovely days. In her mind, the sun was always shining and her parents were always smiling. It was her best memory of them.

Josey took Maud's advice about her clothes. It wasn't hard to do—Maud had an instinct about what was right for her. And Josey was ready to break out, experiment a little. Once, she had delighted in pretty clothes, make-up, even parties ... Then, she had been savagely blighted and it had taken a long time to heal herself. Five long years as John's secretary, hiding from the world. But now, she was ready to live again—very cautiously, one step at a time.

But living again didn't mean putting up with Maud's matchmaking schemes. So far, Maud hadn't advanced any, but she did encourage Josey to get out, enjoy herself. Right now, Maud had no work for her, which was plausible, since Maud was a best-selling writer of historical romances, and the early pages of her book were mapped out in private.

However, just to be on the safe side, Josey

accepted an invitation for dinner from a young man she had met on the plane. Brian Marsden was a dentist who lived in Savannah but told her he was often at Hilton Head, because his parents lived there. He was pleasantly nonthreatening, and although Josey did not consciously use the word 'manageable', it was in the back of her mind when she had agreed to have dinner with him.

Her date was like Brian himself—pleasant but unexciting. Maud might scoff but it was all Josey wanted in her contact with men. During dinner, he told Josey something about the island she was on. It was situated in an area teeming with history, halfway between Charleston, Savannah and Beaufort. They were all old cities, with beautifully restored areas, and active preservation societies. The island had been the hangout of pirates. They had cruised among these waters, wintered on these islands and perhaps buried their treasure in these sands. Captain Kidd, Blackbeard, Anne Bonney—the old names evoked the magic of childhood.

Josey's first intimation that things had changed came the next morning, as she returned from an early tennis lesson at Maud's club. She strode down the driveway briskly, then stopped at the sight of Theodore, washing a silver-grey Mercedes.

Theodore, like Annie, had worked for Maud for years, and like Annie, his job couldn't be defined, except that it included a little of everything. A little chauffeuring, a little gardening, and turning his hand to anything else the occasion demanded. He kept Maud's car in tiptop condition but this wasn't hers.

Josey stared, stricken by a sudden premonition.

Theodore shook his head disapprovingly when he saw her. 'You better hurry on in, Miss Josey. They're looking for you. Mr Thorne got back about an hour ago.'

'And has already put you to work, I see!' Josey snapped.

Theodore looked at her reproachfully. 'What gave you the idea I mind doing a little favour for Mr Thorne? He's always polite and thanks me and tips when I do something extra—like this.'

And why not? He can afford it, Josey told herself uncharitably as she mounted the steps. The first person she ran into was Annie. The small, apple-cheeked woman was carrying an armful of linen, her grey hair standing on end with excitement.

'Where have you been?' she asked Josey. 'Miss Maud's in a taking. She's been asking for you.'

'Why?'

'Wants you to meet Mr Thorne, I should think.' Annie whisked up the steps.

Josey groaned to herself but was prepared when Maud finally caught up with her. She didn't ask where she'd been—her racket and abbreviated tennis costume spoke for themselves. 'I want you to meet Thorne.'

'You weren't expecting him this soon, were you?'

'He 'phoned me last night and mentioned he would be coming in today,' Maud replied. 'Now, brush your hair.' It was in a braid for coolness and Josey gave it a casual swipe. 'He's in the library,' Maud went on, leading the way. 'He brought one of his secretaries with him—a nice woman, a Miss Pettigru—and he says he has to finish some work before he can socialise. So we won't stay but a minute, dear.'

'Work?' Josey asked curiously.

'I may have to give up the library to him this month, if he stays on.' Maud was looking pleased.

At the door, she turned back and looked again at Josey, at the sunburned nose and freckles, the baby fine curls that had escaped the braid. She untied a sweater Josey had knotted around her waist and flicked it on to a chair.

'You'll do,' she said smilingly. 'Now come on in and meet Thorne.'

CHAPTER TWO

JOSEY followed her reluctantly. Maud's voice had a no-nonsense sound to it.

'Thorne! You're going to have to put that brief down long enough to meet Josey!'

Brief? Josey confusedly absorbed the surprising picture of a room dedicated to work. The usually clean desk in the corner was littered with papers and folders and Josey's typewriter by the window had been taken over by a severe looking woman of uncertain age. The chair behind the desk was empty and it wasn't until Thorne answered from behind them that Josey realised he was in the room and had apparently been pacing the floor while dictating.

'Can't it wait, Maud?' His voice was deep and crisp with impatience. 'I want to get this off in today's mail.'

Josey started, then realised with horror that she knew that voice. She knew this man. His face, his voice were branded forever on her brain. She had dreamed about him in her worst nightmares, and once, she had hated him with a hot, bitter hatred that she had learned to control only after years of self-discipline.

She turned slowly, her mind screaming in protest; expecting to be publicly denounced as a criminal; expecting, at the very least, to receive a puzzled look of half-recognition.

He wasn't even looking at her.

Oh, it was him, all right. Not Thorne

Lorrimer, as she had once thought, but Thorne
Jordan Macallan. Maud's nephew, apparently. It
was the sort of mad, unbelievable coincidence
that one swore could never happen. But it had
happened. The dissolute playboy had turned into
a hard-working lawyer with an outstanding
reputation among his fellow members of the bar.

He was changed, of course. The thick black
hair was sprinkled with a distinguished silver; the
lines on his face were scored a little more deeply
and the cynicism was certainly more pronounced.
He was harder—the thin mouth more contained.

He looked up impatiently, his eyes passing over
Josey with an unflattering lack of interest. 'Can't
it wait, Maud?' he repeated.

'Yes, it can, but I thought you might like to
meet Josey. After all, you two have heard me
speak of the other for years, but you've never
met. Josey,' she went on, 'this mannerless young
man is my nephew, Thorne Macallan. And this is
Miss Pettigru, his secretary. Josey Smith.'

Josey swallowed convulsively but did not
speak. She couldn't. Thorne Macallan, however,
muttered a bored, 'How d'you do,' then added,
'Maud, I've booked a room for Miss Pettigru at
the Hilton. Can Theodore carry her over when
she finishes typing this brief? Say—in about an
hour?'

'Of course, darling.'

They left then, Josey following Maud in a state
of merciful numbness. Did he really not
recognise her? Could it have been a trick? The
possibility that it wasn't a coincidence turned her
ice cold with shock, but a moment's calm
reflection reassured her. No, she had simply
made a colossal, unbelievable mistake. She had

blundered into a friendship with the aunt of her worst enemy. She felt like laughing with relief and crying with the bitter irony of it all.

'What's wrong? You look pale, darling,' Maud said anxiously.

Josey looked at her dazedly. 'Maud, how did I get such a wrong impression of your nephew?'

'Wrong impression?'

'That he was—well—different. Even his name . . .! And I thought he'd never worked a day in his life.'

Maud turned pink. 'Well, as to that, I—er—may have given you that impression,' she said uneasily.

'*Why?*'

'To keep you separated. Josey, Thorne has been opposed to you from the beginning. He has taken the attitude that you were an opportunist and would eventually turn on me, if I allowed it. Why else, he said, would a young girl make a friend of a much older woman? I knew he would soon learn differently if he knew you, but—well, I didn't want him to know you. You were very vulnerable in those days. Thorne is very attractive to women and—you could have been shattered by a bad love affair. Thorne *is* unscrupulous, and you would have been fair game to him. Not that he is—unfeeling—but I was afraid for you,' she finished simply.

Josey listened in frowning silence. Maud had overestimated her nephew's appeal, but of course, she wasn't to know that. Most women would find him devastating. It was just that she was immune. 'Do you think I'm less vulnerable now? Or is he less cynical?'

'No, to the latter question. But you are

stronger. He can't hurt you now. You can hold your own—I am sure of it.'

'Thank you for the vote of confidence,' she said drily.

She left Maud then, and went to her room. In her pretty pale green bathroom, she pressed a wet cloth to her face and tried desperately to quell her uneasy stomach, If Maud only knew, she thought helplessly. Would Maud want her as a secretary— as a friend, even—if she knew Josey was a parolled convict, that even her name was false? Yes, Maud would—but her nephew was something else, altogether.

Why hadn't she listened closely when Maud prattled on about her Thorne? From time to time, she had noticed Macallan's picture in the paper, or his name, in connection with a case, but she had refused to read about him. A capsule biography might have mentioned his connection with Maud, and this could have been avoided. Why, even John must have known him! But her life as John's secretary had been so quiet, so— cloistered, she had not met many people.

Of course, she couldn't stay on now. She was scared to death he would find out who she was: he could destroy her. Not only was she an ex-felon, but she had violated her parole, and could be returned to prison to serve out the remainder of her sentence—another eighteen months. And from what she knew of Macallan, it would give him great pleasure to see to it personally.

Once she had made threats, swore to be revenged. It all seemed so futile now, those dark, bitter thoughts she had nursed in prison. But a clever lawyer like Macallan could use those threats to put her in her place—or what he considered her place.

Looking back, she realised she should never have pleaded guilty when she was innocent, but her lawyer had been very persuasive. And she had been scared and alone, with no family or friends to advise her. When he told her it would be cut and dried; much easier than chancing her fate with a jury trial, and the Judge would be sure to give her a suspended sentence, she had believed him. But neither of them had reckoned with Macallan.

Looking back still further, she saw all the wrong turns she had made, the wrong decisions— beginning with the first one: her decision to leave Medlar's Mill, Alabama, after the death of her parents. But she was talented—she could sing, and she was beautiful. All her friends assured her that Jocelyn Stewart's name was destined to be famous. So she took the little money she had and headed for Atlanta.

She soon found that dreams are not reality and money melts quickly in a big city. Her living expenses were high and in addition, there were voice lessons—her voice did not project well over the noisy babble of a nightclub. She had to buy clothes for her act, and a complete range of make-up. One of the club managers insisted that she become a blonde, So, what with one thing and another, her money was soon gone.

It was about then that she met Tony Leyden, a young man with a seemingly endless supply of cash, and an equal desire to spend it all on her. He set seige to her virtue with gifts, flowers, expensive evenings and little loans from time to time, to 'tide her over'. Josey managed to hang on to her virtue but she was weak when it came to the loans. Sometimes, they paid her rent that week and sometimes Tony gave her the only meal she had that day.

She recognised later that her handling of Tony was stupid, that inevitably, he was going to demand payment for all those favours.

'You damn little tease!' he growled. 'Do you know how much that dinner set me back tonight? What did you think I expected from all those meals and that rent money I advanced you? A run-around?' That was the last night, when Tony became ugly and threatening.

'I never asked you to!' she cried, sickened by her own naiveté. She was humiliated, too, because there was a certain amount of justification in his words. 'I think we'd better stop seeing each other. I'll pay you back as soon as I can, but let's call it quits.'

He had apologised then, and finally succeeded in wringing a promise of another date for the next night. That day, he caught her at her apartment door as she was leaving for work.

'I'd like you to keep this box of mementoes for me,' he explained casually, holding out a shoe box wrapped and tied. 'My landlady snoops and I don't want her prying through my things.'

'Very well.' She had taken it coolly, seeing it as another in a long list of efforts he'd made to involve her in his life. Under the circumstances, however, she could hardly refuse.

'Put it on your closet shelf,' he added, with a quick, nervous smile. 'I'd feel safer if it's up on the top shelf, out of the way.'

That night, when the police came, they had known exactly where to look when they searched

her place. She hadn't taken it in, at first, looking
dazedly at the money—thousands of dollars—
which they said Tony had stolen from his
employer. Because the box was in her possession,
she was taken into custody and arraigned as his
accomplice, her protests ignored. It wasn't until
later that she learned Tony had implicated her in
it all, from the beginning.

Her attorney was sent to her by the Public
Defender's office. He was young, inexperienced,
and from the start, hadn't believed her.

'Did you know Leyden has hired Macallan for
his defence?' he remarked after their interview
was completed and he was ready to go.

'What is Macallan?' she asked dully.

'Not what—who. T. J. Macallan is just about
the most brilliant defence lawyer around.' His
voice was filled with a grudging admiration. 'Not
his usual sort of case—this—but I understand it's
a personal thing. Your boyfriend has got himself
some clout, Miss Stewart.'

She flinched. 'Not my boyfriend.'

He shrugged. 'He can't help but do our side
good, so don't knock it. I understand Macallan is
pressing for an early hearing. Whatever con-
cessions he gets for his client will automatically
be extended to you.'

When she saw Macallan, Jocelyn felt hope—for
the first time. This man would accomplish
something. Thank God, he was on her side!

She watched him greedily, seeing his manner-
isms, the cool smile, the scornful eyes as they
watched her lawyer present her case. Once, he
glanced at her, the grey eyes passing over her
indifferently with a contemptuous lack of interest.
She flushed with mortification. She knew she

looked terrible—the anxious weeks had taken their toll. Her dress was cheap and unattractive, and her bleach was growing out—the dark roots were showing.

She had looked at Tony once, noticing his confident manner. He had avoided her eyes from the beginning. She shrugged tiredly. He was nothing to her now: a piece of dirt, a bit of trash. He wasn't even worth her hatred.

She had no idea that Tony was shocked by her appearance. Gone was the glow, the sparkle, that made him infatuated with her. Her eyes were dull, empty; her slender body skin and bones. He felt righteously that she had betrayed him by becoming so defeated. Why, his lawyer was going to think he was blind to have fallen for her.

The shock of Macallan's betrayal—or what Jocelyn considered his betrayal—was so great that she passed her first weeks in prison in a state of dull apathy. When that passed, she kept herself going by dreaming of revenge. She became a model prisoner by deliberately blanking out all memories—even the happy ones—and living like a vegetable. She made herself eat to stay alive, but she paid no attention to her appearance, beyond cutting her bleached hair as it grew out. She learned to type so she could get a job, and she quietly hated Macallan. At night, her mind rebelled at its rigid daytime discipline and she had nightmares, mostly about bringing Macallan to his knees.

Eventually, she was parolled. Her first interview with a lecherous parole officer gave her a good idea of what her future would be if she didn't co-operate by allowing him sexual favours. She fled from him in horror, back on to the city streets, sure of one thing: she was going to have to change her name and make her own way, if she was going to survive. The other alternative was suicide.

It was in that mood that she stumbled into the city library and met a funny little creature dressed in a World War I aviator cap and a long, flapping car coat, circa 1905. Her mop of silver curls, her bright eyes and twitching nose reminded Josey irresistibly of a small clever toy poodle, wandering among the stacks of books.

That didn't last. Within a short time, she was sitting opposite Maud Lorrimer in a nearby coffee shop, unburdening her difficulties in finding a job. She had introduced herself as Josey Smith and learned, in turn, that Maud wrote novels under the name of Frances Flower. Josey had even read some of them.

She had soothed her conscience about the name by reminding herself that Smith was her mother's name and everyone in Medlar's Mill had called her Josey since the day she was born. And making a clean break with a new name was symbolic, somehow. Jocelyn Stewart had been a fool, a stupid, naïve little idiot who had believed everything she had been told and went to prison for it. Josey Smith was going to be strong and independent, and a lot more cynical about men.

'I have a friend,' Maud said suddenly. 'A dear old fuddy-duddy who has just retired from teaching in a college and wants to write a book. A history book about early Georgia or something equally dull. He needs an assistant who can do research and type. Think you can do it?'

'Doesn't that sort of thing require a college degree?' asked Josey cautiously.

Maud waved airily. 'So what? Lie a little. The job carries room and board,' she added persuasively.

Later, Maud admitted that she had been persuaded to befriend Josey by reading in her horoscope that morning, that she would form a meaningful new friendship that day. It was precisely the kind of impulsive, generous thing Maud would do.

Josey saw John through four long, dull history books. He was nearly through the fifth when he died.

Until then, Josey hadn't looked back. Until now . . .

CHAPTER THREE

JOSEY looked at herself in the mirror. She was still pale, but her eyes had lost that blank look and no one, looking at her, would guess she had just sustained a severe shock.

She was feeling better, too. Perspective is a fine thing, she thought wryly, and examining the problem from the vantage point of six years had given her that. Why get so upset? She had remembered Macallan because their meeting had been so traumatic for her, but obviously, he hadn't the slightest recollection of it. And if she kept a low profile, he wasn't likely to. In fact, she had over-reacted, all things considered.

Of course, she no longer thirsted for revenge. She could even laugh, a little, at that violent, shocked young girl. Oh, it still hurt, naturally, but six years of John's civilised approach to life had made her see things in a different light. That perspective again!

She remembered now the last time she had been reminded of Jordan Macallan. She had seen his picture in the paper, photographed at a charity ball with Eve Sanders, one of its organisers. Josey had paused to read, struck by the sheer good looks of the photographed couple. 'T. Jordan Macallan and Eve Sanders, caught last night as they entered the Hilton for the annual . . .'. She had stopped right there.

She wondered if Eve Sanders was the latest in a long line of Macallan's women. She courted publicity—of the right sort, of course—was the daughter of a State Supreme Court judge, and the ex-wife—No 3 or 4?—of Dolph Sanders, the millionaire sportsman. She was beautiful, but Josey, studying her face, thought she looked arrogant. Obviously, an ideal choice for Thorne Macallan!

Which brought her to Maud, and her absurdity in thinking she could ever be attracted to a man like that. Maudie could rest easy, Josey thought amusedly, leaning forward to apply lipstick.

Her first panicky thoughts about leaving had begun to recede. Thorne wouldn't be staying more than a few days—she could wait it out. At the very least, she could wait and see how it went.

More composed now, she could greet Annie calmly when she knocked on the door a few minutes later. The cook had gone home ill, and she needed help. She knew Josey could cook—would she be willing to help out? Josey would, gladly. It gave her an excuse to hide in the kitchen until she further got her bearings.

She made a quiche, which was one of her impromptu standby meals, but Annie wouldn't hear of her remaining in the kitchen to whip up a salad or dessert. She was as capable as anyone of putting ice cream into a parfait glass and pouring creme de menthe over it, she scolded. Besides, Miss Maud expected Josey for lunch.

'No, she doesn't.' Theodore, wearing a white coat, came into the kitchen. 'Mr Thorne has just told her that as long as he's working on that brief, he'll have his lunch in the library. Miss Maud has taken to her bed. She says she's not hungry.'

Annie's eyes met his. 'Disappointed, is she?'

'Yup. He's a hard man, and he doesn't like

being pushed. She ought to know that.' Which meant exactly nothing to Josey.

Josey's first meeting with Thorne occurred in the late afternoon. She was making flower arrangements in a little room off the kitchen when he suddenly appeared in the doorway. He had changed out of his business suit into a pair of running shoes and well worn jeans that moulded his powerful thighs. He was wearing a baggy sweatshirt, probably one he had in college for there was a scarlet number across the chest. And he looked, in a subtle way, tougher and more dangerous.

'I believe you and I are due for a talk, Miss Smith.' He smiled wolfishly.

She frowned cautiously. 'A-are we?'

'Get a raincoat or something, and we'll take a walk.'

'*Now?*'

'No better time. It won't wait.'

Josey took down an old raincoat that was hanging on a peg, and probably belonged to Annie. There was a scarf in the pocket, which she tied around her head. Her hands were trembling and she thrust them into the pockets as she followed him out the back door and across the lawn. He was headed for the beach by way of a boardwalk that had been put down between Maud's house and the one next door.

The sky was grey and sullen overhead, and Josey saw why he had suggested the raincoat. The trees near the beach were stunted and twisted, some of them into gargoyle-like shapes, and beyond them, a long line of sea oats and the dunes provided a protective cover. But once they were on the beach, the full force of the wind hit them, tearing at the buttons of Josey's raincoat and fluttering her scarf.

Abruptly, she stopped and dug in her heels.

'What's this all about?'

'I brought you out here so we could talk. I didn't think you'd want to be overheard.'

Josey bit her lip. 'Do we have anything confidential to say to one another?'

He looked at her remotely. 'I think so—when it's about Maud.'

Her heart jolted. 'Is Maud really ill?' she half-whispered.

He frowned. 'Of course she isn't ill!' he said exasperatedly. 'Are you going to pretend you didn't know she was faking?'

'No.' Josey was slightly taken aback by his frankness. 'But why do you say faking?' she added quickly. 'Surely you know by now that everything is larger than life with Maud? She may have really thought she was dying, particularly after John Trescott's sudden death. Besides, that's how it is with her. A headache becomes a brain tumour and a faint becomes a heart attack.'

'You don't have to explain my aunt to me, Miss Smith,' he snapped. 'I know her as well as you do. But you must allow me to know the difference between faking and the real thing. After all, I saw her while she was in the hospital, and I talked to her doctor. Maud faked that little drama.'

'Did—she?' she faltered.

'Yes. She did it, partly, to bring me to her side.' He smiled bleakly. 'I had been neglecting her lately. But her real purpose was to get you here. You had refused to come.'

'Yes,' she agreed hesitantly, 'but, you see . . .'

'All too well!' he cut in crisply. 'Obviously, this island is devoid of the sort of opportunities a girl like you craves. It didn't have much to offer, did it?'

She blinked. She wasn't stupid—she had already realised he wasn't friendly—but she hadn't expected a personal attack. She pulled herself together and tried to meet it. 'Perhaps you'd tell me why I agreed to stay, then?'

'Gladly.' He was looking grim. 'She offered you an inducement. Me.'

The man was mad. 'And that kept me here?' she asked incredulously.

'Panting with eagerness.'

She snorted on a gust of mocking laughter. 'I think you flatter yourself, Mr Macallan.'

'No, I know your type.'

'For someone who's known me all of five minutes, you're hardly in a position to categorise me as a type!' she snapped.

'Don't be a fool, Miss Smith. You must know that my aunt has been talking about you to me for years. Mostly as a prospective wife.' He ignored her stunned look of horror. 'She stepped up her campaign when I saw her in the hospital, and I saw then that this meeting was inevitable.'

'I don't believe a word you're saying!' she gasped. 'Maud wouldn't do something like that!' But she knew, with a sinking heart, that Maud would. Hadn't she done the same thing to her? Except—not the same. Something here didn't make sense.

He was looking at her cynically. 'Miss Smith, for years I've done everything possible to avoid you. You'd be surprised at how many of Maud's little dinners I've had to be back out of, when I learned you'd be there.'

She burst out laughing—she couldn't help it. In spite of her embarrassment, she could not restrain her amusement at the tactics Maud had used to keep them apart.

'I'm glad you think it's funny!'

She managed to swallow her laughter and the merriment died slowly in her eyes. 'I'm sorry. I don't think you'd appreciate the joke.'

'I'm sure I wouldn't. Are you trying to cloud the issue?'

'And what is that? Maud's matchmaking tendencies?' Her lips twitched. 'You take yourself too seriously, Mr Macallan. Continue to employ those evasion tactics—they've worked so far.'

His eyes chilled to ice and he looked at her with distaste. 'Don't be cute!' His voice was so cutting that she flushed. 'I want you out of here by tomorrow morning at the latest! My aunt is very fond of you—too fond—and I don't intend for you to abuse her confidence.'

Josey drew a sharp breath. 'What makes you think I'd do that?'

'Your past record!' His lip curled. 'You forget, I've listened to Maud talk about you for years. And one fact has emerged—you are an ambitious woman of the particular type I despise.' It's mutual, buddy, she thought viciously, then he knocked her back on her heels. 'Then, of course, there's your manipulation of John Trescott.'

'What do you mean?' she snapped.

'I went by the Trescott home recently, hoping to talk to you, to discuss this—obsession—of Maud's with you, perhaps even gain your co-operation. Instead, I found the Trescott sisters, who asked for my advice as a lawyer. I had to admit, after listening to them, they had a legitimate grievance. They were his only relatives yet he left his estate to you. Fifty thousand, wasn't it? They can't hope to maintain that house on their small income so they'll probably lose it. How will you enjoy your money, Miss Smith, knowing it comes to you at the expense of two old women who have been left homeless?'

Josey was stunned by this hailstorm of half-truths. The trouble was, knowing the truth, she had not taken the old women seriously. They were not destitute—they were merely misers. John knew that. His lawyer had wanted to threaten them with a suit for slander to stop their talk, but Josey had held back, filled with a reluctant sort of pity. And this was where it had got her!

She opened her mouth to explain, then closed it again. If Thorne Macallan accepted her explanation, which was doubtful, he would want proof, and she was damned if she would give him the satisfaction!

'I wasn't aware you were the type of man who listened to the gossip of old women,' she said sweetly.

A muscle clenched in the corner of his mouth. He didn't like that, she saw triumphantly. 'As a lawyer, I have to listen to a lot of people whom I may not personally admire,' he said evenly. 'You will be relieved to know that I told them they hadn't a chance of bringing a suit. John Trescott had a right to leave his money to his mistress if he wished to.'

Ah, he could be cruel! Apparently, the gloves were off. Josey glared furiously at him. Her voice was gritty with anger as she said, 'I hope you don't repeat any of that to Maud. She has a tremendous loyalty to John, and she wouldn't appreciate you slurring his memory, quite apart from what you've implied about me.'

'I have no intention of repeating any of this to Maud.'

'No, I suggest you don't. If you did, you'd find she knows all about John's bequest and approves of it.'

'That was clever of you, but then, I'd never accuse you of being stupid,' he murmured drily.

'Whereas you,' she went on coldly, 'have been quite stupid. By putting my back up, you've made me quite determined not to leave. Goodbye, Mr Macallan.' She turned to go.

He gripped her arm. 'Not so fast. We haven't finished.' She raised her eyebrows haughtily, but his grip tightened. 'You might as well leave, Miss Smith. There's nothing for you here. In a big city, with your looks and money, you could make a good marriage, if that's what you want. Perhaps even a brilliant one. Not every man is as fastidious as I am,' he added deliberately.

'Please remove your hand, Mr Macallan,' she said icily.

He dropped his hand and hooked his thumbs in his belt loops. 'I suppose you're waiting for me to make it worth your while,' he said dryly. 'Very well. How much?'

'Why, Mr Macallan, are you trying to bribe me?' she asked sarcastically.

'You're damned right I am.'

'And you think money will make me leave Maud?'

'If the price is high enough,' he retorted coolly. 'How much?'

She paused, savouring her reply. 'Hmm. Another fifty thousand will give me a nice round sum in my bank account.' She looked at him expectantly, her eyes wide with innocence.

'You must be mad! Or unbelievably greedy!' His face hardened. 'You're not serious?'

'You are *so* discerning, Mr Macallan,' she cooed.

'So you had no intention of leaving—or it's some sort of blackmail scheme to extort money from me? I'll warn you, Miss Smith, try that sort of thing and I'll see you put in jail.'

She slapped him then—to her astonishment. It was an instinctive reaction to his mention of jail. She had always abhored violence and since her term in prison, she had found any form of it sickening. She had seen it break out there over something as unimportant as a pack of cigarettes. But his contemptuous way of riding roughshod over her feelings plus his mistreatment of her in court had finally goaded her into losing her temper—something she had sworn not to do. She exulted in the thrill of primitive pleasure it gave her even as she watched with fascinated terror as the imprint of her palm spread across his face.

He stared at her without flinching, his eyes deadly with rage. 'You little bitch.' His mouth barely parted. 'Do that again and I'll make you regret it.'

She flung her head up defiantly. 'Don't think I don't know what's wrong with you, you hypocrite!' she cried. 'You're scared to death Maud will change her will in my favour!'

His face darkened. 'So that's it! His eyes glittered at her. 'Having fleeced John, you're after Maud! You greedy little tramp, I'll ruin you first!'

She swung at him again, but this time, he caught her hand before it made contact. Exerting pressure, he twisted it cruelly behind her back, bringing her almost to her knees. 'I told you I'd make you regret it if you tried to hit me again!' he said softly. 'Promise to behave and I'll let you go.'

She glared at him. 'Go to hell, you basta . . .' The words broke off as he twisted viciously, and she blurted out a cry of agony. 'L-let me go!' He released her slowly.

'You're going to hear me out, Miss Smith,' he said grimly. 'I have no intention of allowing you to victimise my aunt. I know all about you.' He smiled coldly at her expression. 'Oh, yes, she told me all about how she met you and sponsored you to John Trescott. It was a damned stupid thing for her to do, for she didn't know a thing about you, except that you had crawled into her life like a street-wise little alley cat!'

Her eyes deepened until they were tawny points of fury. She was beyond all caution now, her heart and mind closed to everything but bitter memories of the past. 'I have no intention of obliging you by leaving Maud! And your threats and insults don't scare me, either! You're a liar and a bully and a dishonest lawyer, Mr Macallan, and you're a sadistic coward, too! You should be disbarred!'

'My legal reputation is something I don't have to prove to you,' he said indifferently. 'So keep your filthy little tongue out of my affairs.'

'Your legal reputation isn't worth two cents if you betray your clients as you did—s-someone I know!' she raged at him.

He frowned. 'What are you talking about? Who? I want an explanation of that particular piece of slander.'

Josey was jerked out of her rage by a belated sense of caution. 'I don't have to explain anything!' She met his frown bravely.

'You damned well do! Are you trying to blackmail me? Or, are you merely throwing out wild accusations at random?' he added contemptuously.

Her temper flared again. 'Oh, no, not at random!' she said harshly. 'I *know* from personal experience that you're a liar; a filthy shyster lawyer who uses every slimy little legal trick in the book to distort the truth! But I can fight dirty, too. I'm an alley cat, remember?'

'You're hysterical,' he said coldly.

By now, she was spitting with rage. She even resembled the alley cat he had likened her to. Her eyes were narrow golden slits. Her hair had pulled loose from her scarf, and stood on end, glittering with copper fire. 'I'm fighting mad, Mr Dirty Lawyer Macallan!' She choked on a sob of fury and raised a hand to dash away a tear of rage. 'You've insulted me and questioned my love for Maud, and I *won't* stand still for it any longer! This is one alley cat who isn't going to lay down dead just to please you! In case you haven't got the message, I'm not ever going to let you push me around again!'

He stared at her frowningly, his black brows shadowing his cold grey eyes. She cast him one more fierce look of loathing, then turned and began to run clumsily back across the dunes.

It had begun to rain and the water mingled with Josey's tears. She didn't notice. Sobbing wildly, she stumbled on, unaware that he watched her with a flat, unwavering stare until her figure disappeared behind the trees.

CHAPTER FOUR

'WHY did you do it, Maud?'

Josey had rushed to Maud's room as soon as she got in to demand an explanation. She hadn't stopped, except to strip off her raincoat, and she was in no mood to be put off. But Maud made her wait and get a towel from the bathroom, then dry her hair before she would discuss it. Finally, she put her book down deliberately and peered at Josey over her spectacles.

'Did it work?' she enquired with interest.

'*Work?* I've just had a knock-down, drag-out fight with your nephew! I slapped him and he nearly broke my arm!'

'Then it worked,' Maud said with relish.

'What are you talking about? Maud, be serious! Thorne and I *hate* one another! He asked me to leave—no, he *told* me to leave! I wouldn't be surprised if he left himself, if I don't.'

'Oh, no, he won't leave. He's too stubborn.' Maud was looking amused. 'He promised to stay through the holidays and he'll stay—to spite you, if nothing else. He may try to force me to get rid of you, but I shall cry and have heart palpitations . . .'

'That won't fool him!' Josey said scornfully.

'Of course not,' Maud returned calmly. Then she grinned wickedly. 'Oh-h! He must be infuriated!' she exulted.

'That's another thing. What have you been saying to him, Maud? From what he told me, you've been throwing me at him as a—a marriage partner. *Why?*'

'It seemed the best way to keep you two apart,' Maud murmured. 'He hates being pursued.'

'Thanks a bunch,' Josey said bitterly. 'Couldn't you have just told us both the truth? Why, now, are you trying to throw us together? Maud, are you plotting something?'

'Yes,' Maud admitted. Her eyes were a guileless blue.

'If that means what I think it does, I can tell you I wouldn't marry your precious nephew if he was the last man on earth. I despise him! No, I—I *hate* him!'

Maud chuckled.

'I'm leaving tomorrow, Maud. I'm quitting and going back to Atlanta.'

Maud yanked off her glasses and glared at her. 'Oh, no, you aren't, Josey Smith!' she said darkly. 'You're going to stay and see this thing through!'

'Sorry, Maud, but not even for you will I stay in this house and put up with that man.'

'You're staying! You *owe* me one, Josey, Smith!'

There was a long pause. 'Yes, I guess I do,' Josey said bleakly. 'But I never thought you'd call in the debt, Maud.'

Maud flushed. 'Okay, so I'm a bitch for putting it on that basis,' she admitted defiantly. 'But this is something that means a lot to me. You're going to have to stand up to Thorne and not let him intimidate you. In other words, I'm counting on you to slug it out with him.'

Josey's mouth twisted. 'That's hardly an incentive to marriage,' she commented dryly.

'Oh, I don't expect you to *marry* him!' Maud sounded surprised. 'I mean—you and Thorne? Well, *really*, it would be like mixing oil and water. All that pressure I put on him when I was in the hospital was just to—er—ginger things up a bit. It created an atmosphere of intrigue. No, all I want from you, Josey, is one small favour. I want you to shake him loose from a man-eating shark he's tied up with.'

'A man-eating shark?' Josey repeated blankly. 'Are you—do you mean—a *woman*?'

'You might say that. A very predatory female, anyway.'

'And I'm supposed to take this predatory female's place in your nephew's bed?' Josey asked drily.

'Lord, *no*!' Maud looked horrified. 'I just want you to put a spoke in her wheels. By now, Thorne should be finding you a challenge—you see—he's not used to a woman who says "no".' Maud's eyes twinkled. 'This woman is extremely possessive. I'm counting on her jealousy to cause trouble between them. It's tailor-made, Josey! And hating him as you do, you shouldn't mind making trouble for him.'

'I don't like the set-up,' Josey said bluntly.

'Where's your fighting spirit?' Maud demanded.

'I think I left it on the beach,' Josey smiled weakly. Her words seemed to indicate an acquiescence of sorts and Maud's eyes brightened.

'Josey, dear, the last thing in the world I'd want is for you to get hurt, but you don't like the man. This woman, Eve Sanders, is here now. She came with him this morning and has got a suite at one of the hotels. She practically forced me to invite her to dinner—I told you, didn't I, that she was clever—although I made it clear that she wasn't welcome. But she's persistent and thick-skinned where he's concerned, and I'm afraid he'll drift into marriage with her.'

'He's succeeded in remaining a bachelor so far.'

'Yes, but she means to have him. Dolph Sanders had no intention of proposing, either, but he found himself married to her. She knows I hate her, and she has taken pleasure in hinting that after they're married, she'll separate Thorne from me.' She added desperately. 'Josey, he changes when he's with her. She appeals to the cold, cynical side of his nature.'

Josey was sympathetic. She saw Maud's problem. But this sort of thing was out of her league. 'Maud, I'm no *femme fatale*. In a fight between this woman and me, I'd be outclassed. Besides, I'm all out of shark repellant,' she added whimsically.

'Josey, in a fight between Eve and you, I'd put my money on you anytime,' Maud replied. 'This isn't going to be a woman against woman thing. I've set you up to fight Thorne.'

'Why?' Josey asked bluntly.

'Let's just say it's an experiment, and leave it at that, shall we? Just be honest in your feelings towards him and let nature take its course. You don't want him to think you're afraid of him, do you?'

It was that last remark that did it. On her way back to her room a few minutes later, Josey reflected wryly that Maud was a very respectable amateur psychologist.

Of course, there was one confession she hadn't made to Maud. It could blow the whole thing up and ruin all of Maud's plans, which seemed to consist mostly of allowing Eve's jealousy make a fool of her. Josey shrugged. It sounded rather fanciful to her.

So far as she was concerned, she was standing her ground. If Thorne Macallan recognised her, she'd hire a lawyer to defend her case of parole violation. And she'd find one just as smart and ruthless as Macallan. She wasn't running scared any longer.

She walked into her room before realising it was occupied. Macallan was standing beside her bed, examining a picture of John and Maud that she kept on her bedside table. She had snapped it herself last summer in the garden. She remembered the day vividly, and the happy smiles on the faces turned towards her.

He replaced the picture casually, as though he had a perfect right to be there. She stared at him stonily, aware of every single thing about him. He had changed out of his wet things into a shirt and slacks, and his thick, black hair gleamed wetly in the lamplight. The face he turned towards her wore a hard, questioning look, and he examined her face as though he was seeing it for the first time.

'Great view,' he said blandly, indicating the window. 'Maud must want you to stay. She gave me a room overlooking the neighbour's greenhouse.'

Josey ignored the taunt. 'What are you doing here?' Her eyes lit on an open drawer. 'I believe you've been searching my things!' she gasped.

'I was waiting for you.' His smooth voice didn't give a thing away.

'And amused yourself by prying through my things!' she snapped. 'What were you looking for? Love letters from John?'

A dry smile flitted across his face. 'Something like that. Maybe I was just looking for an explanation for that piece of histrionics on the beach.'

Her soft mouth hardened. 'Are you referring to my refusing a bribe?'

'I'm referring to that personal attack you made on my integrity.'

'Oh?' she purred. 'Did that bother you?'

'You know damned well it did,' he said cheerfully. 'No lawyer likes to be called corrupt.'

'I didn't call you corrupt, Mr Macallan, although I must admit that's a thought. I think the word I used was dishonest,' she added silkily. 'To deliberately lie for the purpose of having a defendant judged guilty may be a common practice among you lawyers, but I consider it dishonest, especially when the defendant is innocent.'

He had been listening closely. 'I almost never see an innocent defendant, Miss Smith. No matter what you might think, the police are usually very efficient in their jobs. But that's beside the point. I defend, not prosecute. And you're speaking of a prosecution situation. Obviously, you've confused me with someone else. Also, you have a sharp little tongue which I shall enjoy clipping if I hear any more libellous slander.'

'That knife cuts both ways, Mr Macallan,' she said slowly. 'You slandered me, too. We shall both have to be careful.'

He laughed. 'Oh, stop the Mr Macallan stuff.

It's too formal for sworn enemies. Make it Thorne.'

She shrugged.

'Who is this mysterious defendant? A father, a brother . . .?'

'I don't have to tell you that.'

'Are you sure he even exists?' he asked smoothly.

'Why should you think h-he doesn't?'

A cold smile touched his lips, a smile of calculated cruelty. 'It might be a ploy to pique my interest.'

'Can't you get it through your head that I don't want your interest?' she said angrily. 'I learned all I wanted to know about you a long time ago! I despised you then and I despise you now. So keep your interest for your constant companion, Eve Sanders!' she added scornfully.

'Eve Sanders?' He added drily, 'So Maud has been talking, has she?'

'Yes, she has, but I assure you, I'm not plotting to entrap you. The trouble with you, Thorne Macallan, is your ego,' she added deliberately. 'Any woman you meet is fair game, and you automatically assume you can make her your lover. It may come as a shock to you, but I am the exception. You don't appeal to me and you never would, not in a million years. All I want from you is to get out of my room and leave me alone. Permanently.'

His face darkened and a smile of anticipation tightened it into a cruel mask. 'You're a fool, my dear. You've issued a challenge I can't ignore, not with my ego—and not in a million years,' he added mockingly. 'Let's see if you can make it good.'

Too late, Josey remembered Maud's words, and realised she *had* been a fool. He was going to kiss her—she had practically asked him to. He pulled her into his arms and studied her dismayed face impersonally. His arms prevented her recoil, holding her so close she couldn't move.

His breath fanned her cheek as he murmured, 'I am sceptical of all that ranting and raving about a mysterious defendant, and the revulsion you apparently feel for me. I think you want me to make love to you.'

'Why, you conceited . . .!' She had flung back her head, glaring, before she saw, too late, that he was grinning. She had fallen into a trap.

'A temper, too. A temper to match that hair.'

He did not kiss her at once. Watching her from beneath lowered lids, his hand moved slowly across her body until it reached a soft, rounded breast. She drew a sharp gasp as his fingers found the sensitive peak and teased it into a hard, tingling bud. She wanted to struggle, but sensed that to do so would unleash the dark feelings that were waiting just beneath the veneer of sophisticated amusement. 'Very wise,' he murmured mockingly.

Standing there in his arms, her heartbeat a muffled thud in her ears, she waited in frozen silence as he explored her face with warm, questing lips. Her senses registered everything about him—from the quickened sound of his breathing to the heady male odour of his after-shave lotion blended with a salty tang from the sea. She wondered if he was tasting the sea on her skin, too, as he wandered across her cheek to the edge of her mouth, where he stopped to lick her lips. They opened involuntarily, and he kissed her.

She had been kissed before, but never with such assurance and never by a man so confident of his masculinity. Their breaths mingled as he explored the warm, soft sweetness of her mouth. Every nerve in her body sprang into tingling life; her skin bloomed; and there was an incredible sensitivity in the nerve endings of her mouth. She was clinging blindly to his neck when she was suddenly aware that he had released her and was speaking.

'Let me lock the door.'

She jerked away, a red tide of embarrassed colour staining her cheeks. He was watching her with cool speculation. She felt humiliated, degraded. She fumbled for something to say to erase that raw triumph from his eyes.

'I'm sorry but not even for Maud's sake, will I allow you to seduce me,' she said primly.

His face hardened. 'Are you saying Maud put you up to—this?'

A chill feathered along her spine at the savage look on his face. 'N-not exactly. I—I . . .'

'We can't disappointment Maud, can we?' he broke in harshly on her stammered response.

This kiss was different—brutal, even contemptuous. Crushing her mouth beneath his, he forced it open with his teeth, mangling her lips. She fought to free herself but he used his hard strength to quell her, keeping her immobile while his fierce tongue plundered her mouth with assured ease. Tomorrow, she was going to have bruises. Some element of common sense told her to stop struggling and she stood quietly until he released her, pushing her away from him savagely.

She went at him then, her hand darting, fingers curled into claws, aiming for his cheekbone. He caught her by the wrist before it could descend.

'Try that again, bitch, and I'll knock you down!' he promised thinly.

'I hate you!' she sobbed.

He smiled cruelly. 'And you know what I think about that.' With hard knuckles, he forced her soft chin up until she met the bitter triumph in his eyes. 'Tell Maud for me it worked,' he said sardonically. He was barely keeping his temper leashed behind whitened lips. 'I want you,' he said deliberately. 'You're not the exception, as you boasted. Far from it. I can take you anytime I like, and make you like it. But it will be when *I* choose, not at Maud's choosing or yours. When *I* decide, Josey Smith, I'll become your lover.'

'I'll see you in hell first!' she snarled.

He smiled slowly, relishing her furious frustration.

'Almost certainly,' he drawled appreciatively. 'It should be a devilishly fine coupling. Tell Maud that, so she'll remember the next time she's tempted to play God.'

He turned and walked out of the room.

After a while, Josey moved slowly, almost as though she was unsure of the strength in her legs. Going to the closet, she pulled out the first dress she came to and flung it on the bed. Then, she moved unsteadily to the bathroom, where she peeled to the skin and stepped under the shower.

The sting of hot water on her face and body brought her back to life. She stepped out and reached for a towel. She had regained a little of her old fighting spirit but she knew nothing was going to restore her to the proud woman she had been before Thorne Macallan showed her a new side to herself.

For someone with Josey's cool dignity, Thorne's shocking assault on her senses had been an assault on her self-esteem. She had spent many long, hard years building up her defences, shoring them with bitter self-denial until she had thought her citadel was invincible. But now, in the space of a few short minutes, Thorne had torn them down. He had destroyed her image of herself as a strong woman, one who could withstand any pressure. He had made her face her own sensuality and he had done it brutally, damaging her pride and self-respect. Even if he had not been her mortal enemy, even if he had been a man she liked and respected, she would have been shaken to the depths of her soul. As it was, she was devastated.

She wouldn't tell Maud, of course: it would hurt her too much. She didn't think Thorne wanted her to. In spite of his harsh words, he loved his aunt. No, this was her battle, to fight alone.

She returned to her bedroom and saw that she had chosen her oldest dinner dress. It was a rusty brown velvet dating from her early years with John, when she hadn't cared what she bought so long as it was cheap. It suited her mood now. She slid the straight, severe little dress over her head and belted it at the waist. She was in the habit of wearing a lace collar with it—one of her grandmother's—and she searched for it automatically. She had no idea that the creamy old lace was so flattering to her skin, nor that the brown velvet toned with her tawny eyes and copper tinted hair. She applied her lipstick listlessly—a bronze gloss—and gave a final, uninterested glance in the mirror. All she was looking for was the secret she was afraid might be revealed in her eyes: she did not see that she looked like a beautiful, crushed angel.

CHAPTER FIVE

THORNE and Eve were alone, occupying one of the living room sofas. He rose slowly as Josey entered, his eyes studying the proud face before lingering with a trace of satisfaction on the bruised lips. He was a picture of sartorial elegance in a black dinner jacket and a crisply tailored shirt front.

'Good evening, Josey,' he said suavely. 'I'd like for you to meet Eve Sanders. Eve, this is Josey Smith, Maud's secretary.'

'Hullo,' Eve drawled indifferently. She had been sitting so close to Thorne a paper couldn't have been inserted between them, but there was no trace of embarrassment as she studied Josey covertly, her eyes narrowing on the swollen fullness of her lips. Leaning forward, she exposed a gaping cleavage as she handed her glass to Thorne.

'Freshen my drink, won't you, sweetie?'

His face did not change expression but Josey knew instinctively that he hated that word 'sweetie'.

'As soon as I've got Josey a drink,' he said curtly. 'What will you have, Josey?'

'Oh, a spritzer, please.'

'A spritzer! What's that?' Eve raised her eyebrows.

'White wine and soda,' Thorne explained briefly.

'Oh. A sort of poor man's champagne,' Eve said disdainfully.

Perhaps she hadn't meant to be insulting—or perhaps she had, Josey thought, meeting the ice-blue eyes. There hadn't been a trace of friendliness on that beautiful face. Apparently, Eve's sense of possessiveness, which Maud claimed was developed to a fine instinct, was already at work. She was subtlety warning Josey off.

As a matter of fact, Josey's appearance had shocked Eve. She had heard a vague mention of Maud's secretary, but she visualised an older woman, and had been looking forward with anticipation to dazzling Thorne with her beauty. She hadn't expected competition.

She had over-dressed for the occasion—a skilfully draped blue silk that moulded her superb figure and boasted a plunging neckline. She hadn't been able to resist wearing some of the loot she had retained after her divorce from Dolph Sanders—earrings, necklace and a tiny watch encrusted with diamonds. Eve was very confident of her powers—she was sure that her brains, breeding, plus a father who was a judge, was going to get her Thorne Macallan, whom she wanted badly.

Dolph had disappointed her. He had been a hard-drinking, womanising millionaire. She was determined that her next marriage would not be the humiliating experience the first was. She wanted a man whose virility was assured—he wouldn't have to prove it with a constant turnover of lovers. She wanted, in effect, Thorne Macallan.

She knew Maud was her enemy and she was determined to get rid of her after her marriage. For now, she was going slowly although she had hinted to Maud that things were going to change.

But she was prepared to remain at Hilton Head until Thorne left, even if it meant enduring Maud's snubs and insults. Now, she knew she had been wise to come. Josey was Maud's secret weapon.

Thorne did not return to the couch, but dropped into a chair. Eve's lips tightened but she kept up a bright spurt of conversation until, after a few minutes, she rose and sauntering over to his chair, draped herself across the arm. Putting a beautifully manicured hand on his shoulder, she leaned forward to drawl seductively, 'Darling, please don't work tonight. It's our first night here, and I want you to take me back to my hotel early. I promise not to keep you *too* late,' she added, whispering something in his ear.

He looked at her impassively. 'Sorry, my love,' he said blandly. 'I've a stack of work to finish tonight. After dinner, I'll have Theodore drive you back.'

'Why did you ask me to dinner then, if you intended to work?' Eve pouted.

'As I recall, you asked yourself,' he replied coolly. 'I did warn you, you know, that this would be a working holiday for me, when you decided to come. But you assured me you had plenty of friends on the island who would keep you amused.'

Her smile slipped a little and she turned petulantly to Josey. 'What sort of work do you do for Miss Lorrimer?' she asked shortly.

Josey started, disconcerted to have the attention focused on herself. 'I type Maud's letters and her manuscript—when she'll allow me to.'

'When she'll allow you to?' Eve repeated

amusedly. 'Are you saying she won't let you touch her work?'

Josey's eyes met Thorne's, then slid away. 'Not yet,' she said briefly.

To her surprise, Thorne answered her look. 'Maud needs Josey, Eve,' he said deliberately.

'I wonder if she does?' Eve questioned sweetly. 'It sounds to me that Miss Smith's life here is one long holiday. And she draws a whopping big salary at the same time!'

Thorne shrugged, but Eve was satisfied. She had planted a seed: she could do nothing now but wait for it to take root. Thorne wouldn't like this girl taking advantage of his aunt. Inevitably, he'd begin to wonder why she was here, and see through his aunt's scheme. He wasn't a man to take kindly to being managed by a woman, even if it was his aunt.

Turning to Josey, she began to question her sweetly about her work background, her qualifications, and finally her personal background. Josey answered her briefly, gradually resenting the impertinence.

'And your parents?' Eve asked. 'Didn't they object to you leaving home and living with John Trescott—at your age?'

'No. They were dead.'

'Oh. In Atlanta or . . .?'

'I came from a little town in Alabama, Mrs Sanders.'

'You must have been frightfully young to be on your own. Or perhaps you weren't on your own?' she added delicately.

Josey looked at her frowningly, seeing the spite behind the innocent questions. This was the sort of thing she had been getting from Thorne all afternoon, and she was damned if she was going to take it any longer!

Drawing a deep breath, she asked blandly, 'Let's see, *Mrs* Sanders, are you a widow—or divorced?'

'I'm divorced, if that's any of your——'

'Oh-h!' Josey cooed. 'I'd love to hear the details! Were you sexually incompatible? Did you quarrel? What about? How much did you receive in your divorce settlement?'

Thorne choked.

'I suppose you think that's funny!' Eve snapped, glaring at Josey. 'It's not! It's crude and considering your circumstances, a wee bit stupid! Thorne has a perfect right to question you regarding your qualifications, whereas you . . .'

'I have already satisfied myself regarding Josey's qualifications, Eve,' he interrupted in a hard voice. 'You have been too busy on my behalf. I don't need a spokeswoman, but if I should happen to need you, I will let you know. You won't have to volunteer.'

Eve flushed dully and bit her lips. Thorne had never had to put her in her place before, and she realised that she had overstepped that invisible line that she had recognised from the beginning of their acquaintance. Jealousy had made her insecure, and insecurity had made her forget her caution. She was determined to be on her best behaviour for the rest of the night if it killed her.

'Hello, darlings! Have I kept you waiting?'

It was Maud, looking thoroughly pleased with herself. Dressed to the nines in a glittering blue georgette, she wafted into the room on three-inch heels, waving a cigarette holder. Maudie, who never smoked! She dazzled the eye, for she was hung with jewellery, including the bracelet she claimed had been given to her by the Aga Khan and a diamond and sapphire necklace that was supposedly the gift of a certain sheik.

They all stared but it was Eve who exclaimed, with a hint of a catch in her voice, 'Miss Lorrimer! What gorgeous jewellery!'

Maud looked pleased, but Josey was uneasy. Maud was in costume, of course—not even she could be that vulgar!—but what was she up to?

Thorne rose and escorted her to a chair. There was a ghost of laughter in his voice as he said blandly, 'Late as ever, Maud, but worth every minute of it.'

'Late?' she purred. 'I thought I was on time.'

'No,' he disagreed gravely. 'Theodore has been waiting dinner.'

'Well, he'll just have to wait,' Maud said airily. 'I don't intend to start until you open a bottle of my champagne so I can propose a toast. Get us all a drink, won't you, sweetie?'

Sweetie? Josey saw the light. Annie must have given Maud the information that enabled her to broadly caricature Eve. If Annie had also let her know that Eve was being insulting and offensive, Maud would react predictably.

Eve leaned forward to admire Maud's jewellery.

'It will all be Josey's someday,' Maud said graciously.

Eve's smile faltered. 'Don't you think that's a little—unfair to Thorne's future wife?'

'Oh, dear me, no! Besides, the two facts aren't necessarily exclusive,' she added blandly, evading Josey's warning frown.

'You'll probably change your mind half a

dozen times,' Eve said brightly. 'May I look at your bracelet?'

Maud extended her arm and began to give Eve a rundown on the love affair that had burned up three continents. She followed that with the saga of passion on the desert.

'I've never heard that story told better,' Thorne said admiringly.

'I'm not sure if I should believe her.' Eve laughed uneasily. 'Should I, Thorne?'

His eyes met Josey's in what was a perfect moment of amused camaraderie. 'Believe her. It's better than the truth any day.'

'Speaking of stories,' Maud went on blandly, 'this champagne was sent to me by a man with whom I shared two perfect weeks in Paris. Then, we were parted. He had a wife, you see. That was twenty-five years ago, but every year, I receive a dozen bottles of his best vintage. Lest I forget.' She took a sip, then added, briskly, 'But enough of reminiscing about the past. It's the future that counts.' She lifted her glass. 'To Josey and Thorne, whose futures are irrevocably entwined.'

'Indeed?' murmured Eve frigidly. 'You sound confident.'

'Ah, you see, the stars have foretold it.'

'And who reads the stars, Miss Lorrimer?'

'Madam Zelda is my astrologer.' Maud beamed at the enraged woman. 'She sees a marriage in their future.'

'Perhaps—but not necessarily to each other. I should fire her if I were you, Miss Lorrimer. She's obviously incompetent.'

Josey looked at Thorne. He was frowning at Maud, his good humour gone. Damn Maud's eyes, Josey thought furiously. She might be scoring one on Eve but she is embarrassing me.

'I couldn't agree with you more, Mrs Sanders,' she said crisply.

Eve threw her a look that would have shrivelled a rabbit at ten paces. She was too angry and humiliated to recognise an ally when she saw one.

'I don't imagine we have far to look to find out who introduced you to your astrologer, Miss Lorrimer,' she said significantly.

'Eve,' Thorne drawled boredly. 'Don't be absurd. Maud has been seeing Zelda for twenty years. Which would make Josey's influence begin at a rather precocious age, don't you think?' He rose abruptly and extended his hand to Maud. 'Enough fun and games, Maud. Time for dinner. I'm hungry.'

He was also angry, Josey saw. Of course, Eve had behaved badly but Maud had played her like a trout on a line. And now, she was going to have to pay the piper with her nephew's disapproval. She knew it, too, for she slid into her seat at the head of the table in subdued silence.

Dinner was in the formal dining room with the table set with lace mats and Maud's delicate bone china, sterling silver and fragile stem crystal. Candles and a low, rounded centrepiece of roses added a further elegant note to the table.

Eve murmured her appreciation, a complacent look on her face. Obviously, she accepted the exquisite table as a compliment to herself.

The candles flickered, creating dim shadows and carving harsh lines in Thorne's face. Josey glanced at him once or twice, but for the most part, she kept her head down, her eyes on her plate. There was no place for her in this conversation. Eve had taken it over and with her social flair, it went just where she chose. Which meant that she centred it mostly on herself and Thorne, with an occasional remark to Maud about mutual acquaintances. Maud, mouselike, let her dominate the conversation—which was very unlike Maud. If Josey had been looking at her closely, she might have suspected something from Maud's limpid blue eyes.

As soon as dinner was over, Josey excused herself, saying it had been a tiring day. No one said anything to deter her.

She had not been sleeping well since John's death, but all her nights, placed end on end, could not equal this one. She tossed and turned, and when she finally did sleep, her dreams were haunted, her sleep exhausting. She awakened the next morning with a bad headache and dark circles under her eyes. It was a beautiful rain-washed day, one that would have ordinarily sent Josey joyously to the window, bursting to be outside. But she eyed the scudding clouds in the blue sky with a faintly jaundiced look and dragged herself into the bathroom to brush her teeth.

When she went to breakfast, Maud was alone.

'Good morning, darling!' she chirped breezily. 'Sleep well?'

'Well enough,' Josey answered cautiously.

'Well, what did you think of last night?'

Josey shook out her napkin. 'Do you mind if I have my coffee first?' she enquired ironically.

'Not at all.' Maud pushed the coffee pot towards her and popped bread in the toaster. 'Now, tell me, what *was* your impression of last night?'

'Personally, I thought it was a disaster,' Josey said drily. 'It's not every dinner where the hostess makes a fool of her guest.'

Maud smirked. 'I had to do it, dear. For his sake. And I assure you, it worked! It was worth it to open his eyes to what a bitch that woman is.'

Josey carefully buttered her toast. 'Have you done that?'

'Oh, Josey, you should've been there last night! No, I guess not—it was your absence that triggered the whole thing.'

Josey stared. 'What do you mean?'

'As soon as you left, she said in that cool way of hers that she was glad to see you knew your place and had enough tact to withdraw from the room.'

Josey's eyes opened wide. 'Lord-y!' she breathed. 'She is stupid!'

Maud grinned. 'Thorne hit the roof. Of course, he was already angry with me . . .'

'He's on to you, Maud. He knows exactly what you're up to.'

'Naturally, he does,' Maud said agreeably. '*He* isn't stupid. I knew I couldn't keep him from catching on. But you noticed I was on my best behaviour at the table? So he couldn't blame me when Eve made her snobbish little remark.'

'What happened?'

'He told her off in that cold, sarcastic way of his. She started crying then, but she couldn't move him although she tried every manoeuvre known to woman, including sex.' Maud's eyes sparkled. 'I'm afraid they forgot I was there, in the heat of the moment. I could have told her she was making a fatal mistake when she upstaged you in the beginning. Funny, too, she's the soul of courtesy to Annie and Theodore, but I suppose this is the first time Thorne has seen her out of her own environment.'

'She was jealous,' Josey said dryly, 'and you engineered the whole thing.'

'And her own bad temper did the rest. Anyway, she's gone. He took her back to Atlanta early this morning.'

'He may not come back,' Josey warned.

'Nonsense!' Maud said heartily, but Josey could see she was worried.

Josey was busy the rest of that week. She was terribly restless and she was glad Maud had work to keep her busy. She got jittery if she was idle.

Brian had a free afternoon Wednesday and called to ask her to go sailing with him. Maud insisted that she go. She knew Maud was beginning to worry about her, for she wasn't sleeping well and it showed in her face.

The afternoon on the water was good for her. But when she looked at Brian's pleasant, freckled face, she knew she could never use him as a panacea for whatever was ailing her. She wished desperately that he had the power to heat her blood, make her ache with passion, and her heart beat faster. She would have willingly let him make love to her if she thought he could work some kind of magic formula and turn her thoughts around. But to have sex—and for the first time, too!—with one man merely to chase erotic images of another out of her mind was stupid and self-destructive.

Before they parted, Brian made a date for dinner that night, and she willingly accepted. They parted at the boat, for he still had to lower the sails and turn in his docking pass, and Josey walked home.

When she saw the grey Mercedes parked in the driveway, she knew why she had been so restless. This was what she had been waiting for.

CHAPTER SIX

SHE dressed carefully for her date with Brian, a soft, ruffled amber dress with a swirling hem around her knees. She brushed her hair until it gleamed with highlights and carefully smoothed on a creamy eyeshadow and bronze lipstick. Suddenly, she realised she was dressing for Thorne—she wanted him to see her looking her best and able to attract another man besides him.

Downstairs, she met his eyes with a flare of antagonism. 'Hello,' she said coolly. 'I thought you must be back.'

'Going out?'

She nodded. 'We're trying out a new dance club that just opened on the beach. The Fifth Dimension.'

'Have fun.'

At dinner, she was restless and unable to concentrate on what Brian was saying. When they weren't dancing, her eyes shifted constantly, probing the room relentlessly. Suddenly, her attention was focused on a couple who had just entered and were being shown to a table near the dance floor. Thorne and a beautiful girl—another blonde. Where did he find them, she wondered viciously.

She turned to Brian, a feverish glitter in her eyes. 'I—can we go?' she asked quickly. 'I'm rather tired. I think I had too much sun today.'

He was very solicitous, and she couldn't get out of there fast enough. Her face was hot with

embarrassed colour. She admitted it to herself,
although it made her cringe to realise how
vulnerable she was. She had told Thorne where
she would be, hoping he would come. But she
hadn't been able to sit there tamely when she saw
he was with another girl. She was ashamed when
she realised that she had probably been very
obvious to him.

The next morning, he asked her if she would
like to accompany him to Charleston. When she
hesitated, he added indifferently, 'You'll be on
your own. I'll be in a law office all morning.'

'Do go, Josey,' Maud broke in. 'I ordered a
dress by phone and need someone to pick it up.'

There was no trace of his former antagonism in
Thorne's casual invitation, so Josey cautiously
agreed. Within thirty minutes, they were on their
way. Thorne was a silent driver. The car radio
kept them amused, tuned to a station that was
broadcasting a revival of *Porgy and Bess*. When
they were crossing the Ashley River, he asked,
'Where did Maud say this shop was?'

She gave the number on Church Street.

'Sounds like it's near where I'll be going on
Broad. I'll find a parking place on the street.'

He found one halfway between the shop and
the law office. As he got out, he consulted his
watch. 'Shall we say I'll meet you back here at
noon? That should give you time to get your
errand done and look around a little.'

'What about the parking meter?'

He shrugged. 'I'll pay the fine if I get a ticket.'

She watched him leave her, striding briskly
along with his briefcase in his hand. She
watched ironically as he drew abreast of a
smiling woman, who turned to look back after

he passed her. She had sensed it, too—that sexual charisma that made all women automatically aware of him. Hadn't Eve told Maud that she was going to have him? She wondered how many other woman had started out with that premise and had to eventually settle for a passing affair?

Maud had called ahead so they were expecting her at the shop. She finished that errand in a matter of minutes, then looked around for herself. What she found was demure on the hanger but deliberately erotic on the wearer. Of ivory crépe, it was cut along Grecian lines, with one shoulder bare and no back to speak of. The fabric alternately clung and swayed, moulding a pointed breast or the shadowy cup between her thighs. God knows what it does at the back, she thought nervously, but she couldn't deny its potential effect.

She bought it on impulse without ever expecting to wear it, then returned to the car. Thorne had given her an extra set of keys, so she unlocked the boot and placed her packages inside, then fed the meter. She still had a lot of time, so she walked towards the Battery, noticing the uniquely different architecture of the old houses and their gardens. Some were hidden behind high brick walls, with only the fan leafs of the palmetto showing overhead. Those she could see were small and formal, some with brick courtyards, tubs of geraniums and azaleas and a small, well-pruned tree or two.

When she reached the Battery, she was at the farthest point in the Charleston harbour. From here, she could see the island of Fort Sumter and just beyond it, the Atlantic. There were sightseeing boats leaving from the dock but looking at her watch, she knew she hadn't the time to take one.

He was waiting for her, leaning against the car, his eyes narrowed against the sunlight. Her heart started thumping heavily, and she recognised the mingled feelings of antagonism, fear and attraction she felt every time she saw him. He was not menacing. Since that night, he had been pleasant, but completely impersonal. It was possible she had blown the whole thing up in her mind. She approached him coolly and smiled politely. 'I hope I haven't held you up.'

'Not at all,' he said absentmindedly. His eyes were probing her face intently. 'What about lunch?'

'I—Shouldn't we be getting back?'

'Maud would never forgive me if I brought you back without feeding you. What is your pleasure? Seafood? Chinese? Italian?'

'You make a choice,' she said faintly.

'Seafood, then.'

They found a restaurant across the bridge that looked promising. Outside, a sign advertised that it featured She-crab soup. The building looked like a beached ship, with gangplank, railing and portholes. Inside, it was decorated with gimmicky nautical furnishings, such as telephones hidden in fog horns and ageing mast heads leaning out above the heads of the diners.

They slipped into their seats and Thorne looked around resignedly. 'I'm afraid we're in for it. This sort of place is usually short on good food. Would you like to go somewhere else?'

Josey didn't answer. She was staring, wide-eyed, taking in all the sights. Suddenly, bells jangled and a lifesized wooden captain overhead went through a pantomime of blowing down a tube and turning a wheel.

'We'll stay, then,' Thorne said indulgently.

Their dacquiris were too sweet, and Thorne seemed resigned to what would follow. Josey had ordered She-crab soup and Thorne a seafood cocktail, and both were excellent. Their seafood dinners were delicious, and Josey began to relax as Thorne's attitude mellowed. Overhead, bells jangled and the lurching pantomime went on, but Josey didn't notice. They explored each other's likes and prejudices in music, the theatre, books, even Charleston. Josey was interested in the latter since what she had seen this morning had whetted her desire to see more. Thorne was a member of the National Trust, and he knew a great deal about what was being done to save some of the old buildings from destruction and restore them.

By the time they finished their lunch, Josey was completely relaxed. She hadn't forgotten that he was her enemy but she was prepared to be realistic.

She was still basking in the glow of good intentions when he asked, 'Would you like to see Drayton Hall before we go home?'

Her eyes brightened. 'Is it far?'

'Just a few miles. It's a plantation home that belongs to the National Trust. I'm sure it's open today.'

'I thought cold, calculating lawyers weren't interested in the romantic South,' she remarked smilingly, then could have bitten out her tongue for bringing a caustic note into the conversation.

But he was smiling. 'We are very interested in architecture, and this happens to be a perfect example of Georgian Palladian.'

They turned off the highway, paid their fee at the entrance gate, then followed the road lined with centuries-old oak trees until they came to the house. It stood in lonely austerity, a reflecting pool at its back and the river in front.

They joined a group leaving with a guide. Thorne had already explained that Drayton Hall was empty, but it did not need antique furnishings—the guide's account made its history come alive. Because it had remained in the hands of the same family until it was acquired by the National Trust, it had never fallen heir to the destruction of progress. It had never been wired for electricity, nor had indoor plumbing installed, and it had only been painted twice in its history—the last time in 1865. For students of architecture, it was a treasure trove of information.

Josey listened to the guide talk about its romantic past, which had come to an abrupt end with the Civil War. It had taken three days of systematic stripping to empty it of its beautiful contents when the enemy soldiers came. What the owners could save, they did by parcelling it out among the loyal slaves who remained. When the guide described the lavish, candlelit balls, Josey could almost see the rooms peopled with graceful, dipping couples.

Thorne leaned forward and murmured, 'If you look closely, you may see Scarlett and Rhett.'

She flushed. 'It's silly, I know, but I'm fascinated by stories like that.'

Later, as they were leaving, he asked, 'So you think you'd have liked to live in those days?'

'Not at all,' she said firmly.

'You surprise me,' he said sardonically. 'Most women get nostalgic about the good old days.'

'Not unless they're fools,' she said crisply. 'Life was too hard on women to ever want to return to the past.'

'Hard?' he asked cynically. 'You were put on a pedestal! Admired, petted, adored, protected . . .'

'For the women who lived there, perhaps,' she gestured scornfully over her shoulder. 'But the rest of them lived lives of drudgery. A baby every year, her body and soul owned by her husband. If you ask me, it's you men who miss the good old days. You were on top then, and you've been going steadily downhill ever since.'

'That's the trouble with you feminists, you have no sense of humour,' he drawled, as they reached the parking lot. He unlocked the car and held the door open as she got in. 'You women want to be construction workers and policemen, but if you aren't given preferential treatment, you can't hack it.' He started the motor, his hard, handsome face wearing a sardonic smile. 'As for your equality claim, if you were to start off all the men and women in the world evenly, the men would still demonstrate their superiority.'

'Are you talking about mental or physical superiority?' she asked sweetly.

'Oh, mental, of course. Our physical strength is obvious.'

She drew a sharp breath. 'Too bad we can't test your interesting hypothesis,' she snapped.

'Why can't we?' His eyes glinted mockingly. 'Take this little skirmish of ours, for instance.'

She froze. Suddenly, their half-playful conversation had entered a new, dangerous plane.

'Or would you rather call it a war?' he asked smoothly. 'That I shall win?'

She touched her tongue to dry lips and

laughed nervously. 'I'd rather call it fanciful nonsense.'

'Do you really think I won't have you before I return to Atlanta?' he asked pleasantly, as though the topic was academic.

She flushed. 'I *know* you won't! All I have to do is whisper one word into the ear of the beautiful Mrs Sanders.'

'Too late,' he drawled appreciatively. 'Eve and I are no longer close friends.'

'Was that her idea—or yours?'

'None of your business, Miss Pry,' he replied amiably, then added, 'I don't like possessive women.'

'In other words, you got tired of her, as you do all of your mistresses sooner or later?' she snapped. 'Maud told me the average duration was four to six months!'

'Do I detect a note of sympathy?' He sounded surprised. 'After her treatment of you?'

'She was jealous!' Josey said sharply. 'And insecure. Rightly so, as it turned out,' she added nastily.

He shrugged. 'I assure you, she knew the score. I made no promises, and when a thing is over, it's over.'

'"It" presumably meaning her bed-worthiness?'

He looked amused. 'Her bed-worthiness, as you put it, was never in question. But she had a few bitchy personality traits that I found objectionable.'

'You *must* tell me what they were,' she cooed sweetly.

He grinned. 'Ask Maud.'

She eyed him with sharp suspicion. 'You know that's why Maud set this thing up!'

His grin widened. 'She was rather obvious.'

'And now that you've learned that I'm not trying to trap you into marriage, you're prepared to have an affair with me? I'm surprised you're willing to forego your fastidiousness and overlook the fact that I was John's mistress!' she added angrily, with a total disregard for the truth.

A slight tightening of his mouth was the only indication that her words had made an impression. 'I make it a habit never to discuss my partner's former lovers,' he said coolly. 'Naturally, I expect the same consideration from her. That, plus her exclusive attention, is all I ask or expect so long as the affair lasts.'

She flinched. 'And what do you expect from a wife?' she demanded hotly.

His face hardened. 'I'd be a fool to expect anything from a wife—which is precisely why I'll never get married.'

'I think you're *disgusting*! C-claiming you're going to attempt to seduce me under your aunt's roof . . .'

'Attempt?'

'How do you think Maud would feel if she knew about this?'

'Maud is a romantic and as much an anachronism as that antebellum mansion back there. She believes in love, happy endings, all the modern fairy tales. She would fool herself that her particular dream was coming true—you and I were falling in love and were going to be married. Whereas you and I, my beautiful little sensualist, are realists. We deal in truth; what we can see and hear and feel. The way I make you feel, for instance, when I kiss you or touch your breasts. The way I intend to make you shudder and moan beneath my lips. It will be that, not some sentimental clap-trap called love, that will bring you to my bed.'

She wanted to put her hands over her ears and close out the sound of the harsh, cynical voice uttering words she did not want to hear. She wanted to deny the pulsing excitement in her veins, the erotic images his words brought to her mind. Desperately, she reminded herself who he was, and to never forget it. He had almost destroyed her once—was she going to let him do it all over again?

'Don't say that!' she choked. 'I *hate* it when you say that!'

He didn't reply but abruptly drew into a lay-by along the highway. He turned off the motor, then leaned over her, splaying his hand across her breast. Her body reacted immediately by swelling beneath his palm.

He laughed harshly. 'Do you think liking or hating has anything to do with this? Or this?' His warm lips sought the thundering pulse at the base of her throat. Her desire flared, and she knew he had correctly read the signs in her quickened breathing, the way her hands curled limply in her lap. He slowly unbuttoned her blouse, watching her face closely, but she didn't move. She stared at him blankly, her eyes wide and a molten gold in her white face. 'You're so lovely,' he murmured.

He did not kiss her, but his hands were exquisitely tender on her soft skin, his touch warm and soft. A slight breeze drifted in through the open car window, reaching her heated cheeks, and she blinked, momentarily distracted. She tried to move but her limbs would not obey her.

When one of his hands cupped her thigh and slid tormentingly down its slender curve, she reached out a trembling hand and touched the head at her breast. At the mercy of her own passions and that aching traitor that dwelled deep within her body, she knew she couldn't have stopped him if he had chosen to take her at that moment in the front seat of the car.

Then, suddenly, she was free and he was snapping her bra with a humiliating expertise. 'Let me go!' she whimpered.

'You're quite free.' There was a thread of soft laughter in his voice and she realised just how ridiculous she had sounded.

'Face it, Josey. Whatever this—this hunger is between us, it's not going away until we feed it.'

'No.'

'I want you—very badly. I admit it, and you're a fool and deceiving yourself if you don't admit it, too.' His voice was indulgent, even amused, and she flushed angrily.

'I am not going to make love with you,' she said stubbornly.

'Yes, you are,' he said softly. 'And very soon. But not under Maud's roof, in spite of your claim. I want you where I can enjoy that lovely body at leisure, all night long.' His hand touched her face lingeringly. 'You're mine, Josey, so don't make any more dates with that nice boy, hmm? He's already halfway in love with you and it would be a shame to disappoint him when you already belong to me.'

He started up the engine and drove out of the lay-by. She turned her head away, staring at the scenery, and after a while, surprisingly, she slept.

CHAPTER SEVEN

THORNE did not carry out his threat, although he remained at Maud's house through that week. He was very busy with a case that was being heard in the Charleston courts, and he spent several nights and every day there, working with the firm of lawyers that had been retained by his firm. When he was home, he worked in the library with Miss Pettigru. Josey only saw him occasionally, and then, at meal times.

She refused two dates with Brian that week on the grounds that she was busy. And she kept busy. If Maud had no work for her, she was outside with Theodore. Together, they moved bulbs and one day, she weeded the lawn and in the ground cover of creeping ajuga. As she viciously attacked the crabgrass, it was as though she was attacking those feelings she could not control.

She was not going to let Thorne Macallan seduce her, she declared violently. She wasn't a mindless little fool or a robot he could control. She was a strong, independent woman who had made her own way for years, and she couldn't be taken against her will. Admittedly, she was strongly attracted to him. She knew now it had been that strong attraction that had made her react so explosively in the courtroom. She had thought he was going to save her and instead, he betrayed her. She hadn't the experience to recognise he had merely been doing his job.

She gave a sudden strangled yelp of denial. *No!* It was a betrayal. Maybe it was only a job, too. But what he had done once, he might do again. He had never made any bones about the impermanent quality of his feelings for her. She was merely a casual date, a one-night stand, a girl whom he could appease his hunger for after one night. He had approached her as a girl of experience, who had lived for years with another man. She had not received soft words, flowers, chocolates, nor even his respect, she reminded herself savagely.

She was right to refuse Brian's request for a date tonight for she hadn't wanted another confrontation, but that was the last concession she was going to make. She had said it once—she was saying it again. She was through running scared.

That afternoon, Thorne walked in while she and Maud were having pre-dinner cocktails in the sunroom. He dropped into a chair and smiled lazily at them.

'I'll be returning to Atlanta tomorrow, Maud.' When she made a sound of distress, he said gently, 'Sorry, my dear. I can't put it off. I do have other obligations, you know.'

She tried to smile. 'Will you be back?'

'Oh, yes.' He turned a predatory smile on Josey. 'I was going to ask Josey to go out with me tonight and celebrate the end of my case.'

'Oh, did you win?' Maud asked eagerly.

'Very satisfactorily.'

While they were talking, Josey's mind was busy with sizzling thoughts. So this is when he had planned her seduction, midway between the end of his case and his return to his lady in

Atlanta! She was to be sandwiched conveniently
in the middle, like a quickie hamburger! She
knew what to do, how to get in touch with Brian.
And when Thorne looked at her enquiringly, she
smiled fiercely into his eyes.

'I'm so sorry,' she said deliberately, 'but I've
made other plans. I already have a date—with
Brian.'

'Hmm, too bad. I wonder if I can find someone
at the last minute—too? Perhaps you and Brian
will be my guests?' He was smiling but there was
a dark thread of anger running through his voice,
and she was savagely glad.

'We'd love to but we'd rather be alone. I'm
sure you understand.'

'Oh, I do.' Oh, he was furious! The pale
sea-grey of his eyes had darkened to a black rage,
deadly, promising retribution.

As soon as she could, Josey went straight to
her room and phoned Brian at his parents'
home. He was delighted to learn that she was
able to make their date after all, and they
decided on a movie.

It was pleasant being with blessedly uncompli-
cated Brian. Josey ended up enjoying the movie.
They stopped off for a nightcap afterwards at a
dark little bar and lingered for a while before he
took her home. As they left the bar, she had an
impulse to ask Brian to take her to a hotel where
she could get a room for the night, but she knew
he would wonder—Maud would wonder, and she
wouldn't hear the last of it. Besides, it was a
cowardly cop-out.

The porch light was on as they drove up, and
Josey turned swiftly to Brian. 'Don't see me in,
everyone's asleep.'

She was fumbling with her key when the door opened.

'Come on in, Miss Smith. You must have known I'd wait up for you,' he drawled silkily. His face was in the shadows and all she could see was a tall, looming shape. 'Come into the living room. I want to talk to you.'

She stopped at the stairs and said firmly, 'But I don't want to talk to you. I'm tired and I want to go to bed.'

'That suits me just fine. That's where I intended the evening to end anyway.'

Something in the implacable voice told Josey that he meant it: it was either bed or the living room, so she followed him reluctantly into the big, dimly lit room.

'I knew that's what you intended,' she said nonchalantly. 'That's why I went out with Brian tonight.'

For a moment, amusement gleamed in his eyes. 'You are merely putting off the inevitable, you know. I thought I told you not to go out with that boy again.'

'Since when do I have to do what you tell me to do?'

'You know when, Josey.' His voice was soft but conveyed a menacing note of warning. 'Don't do it again.'

She threw back her head. 'I'll go out with whoever I like!'

'Not while you belong to me.'

'I don't belong to you!' Desperation made her voice harsh and ugly. Suddenly, inspiration came to her. 'I belong to Brian, if anybody. As of tonight.'

He froze, staring at her, his pale eyes blazing.

His mouth twisted into a cold smile. 'You bitch, you're lying,' he said thinly.

'Why should I lie about a thing like that?' she asked steadily. 'Surely a lady is allowed the privilege of choosing her lover for the evening?' The absurd words tripped off her tongue. 'I didn't want you—I wanted Brian. It was as simple as that.'

She shrank back from the ugly expression on his face as he dragged her into his arms and kissed her with deliberate brutality, forcing her mouth with a crude sensuality that was shocking. It was a contemptuous assault, made in an anger that gave him an excuse to use his male strength against her feminine weakness.

She tore herself away and a cold, fierce smile bared his teeth. With one swift movement, he lifted her and carried her over to the sofa, then yanked her zipper open. From beneath his lashes, his eyes gleamed with a predatory glint that warned her not to fight him, for to fight him would be to lose, and to lose would be to submit. Sliding his hands across her shoulders, he cupped her breasts, his thumbs stroking the nipples with slow, sensuous movements. She fought to prevent the treacherous signs of her arousal.

'No, Thorne,' she moaned.

'Don't you like what I'm doing to you?' he asked idly.

He levered her backwards, his long, lean weight bearing her body down to the soft cushions. He kissed her deeply, druggingly, while all the while, his hands continued with their sensual, pleasurable stroking.

'Don't you like it?' he repeated, breathing in her ear.

'Yes.'

'Tell me how much.'

Her long lashes swept down, covering her golden eyes, and she whispered shamedly, reluctantly, 'I like it—very much.'

'Want me to go on?'

'Yes,' she whimpered.

'You're beautiful, you know,' he murmured softly. 'Like fire and ice. Your skin feels like silk, and your mouth tastes like honey. When you blush, your breasts bloom beneath my hand—like this. You're driving me mad, my beauty.' He raised himself and tangled his hand in her copper curls, tilting her face up to meet his. 'Listen to me. I am Thorne and I am the man who you say you hate and despise. But I'm also the man who can make you ache with desire. Remember that next week, while I'm gone. No,' he added drily, running his fingers lightly over her flushed cheeks. 'I'm not going to take you now. I told you, the first time was going to be at our leisure, in bed, where we can enjoy it.'

His eyes were coldly intent on her face as she sat up and pulled her clothes together. She stood up unsteadily, and he helped her, one hand under her arm, then she had to endure the added humiliation of having him walk her to her bedroom door. The hallway was hushed and dark, wrapping them in an intimate silence. At the door to her room, he turned to her.

'I'll see you soon. And, Josey, don't try to run while I'm gone. If you give me the trouble of having to find you, you won't like it, I promise you.'

But she thought about running. The next morning, she was considering it seriously when

she went downstairs to find that Maud had been
ill all night.

'She wouldn't let me tell Mr Thorne before he
left,' Annie told Josey. 'She said he'd stay if I
did, and she didn't want that.'

The doctor came and pronounced it a virus,
which would probably last twenty-four hours,
and leave her weak and listless.

'She isn't a young woman,' he warned Josey.
'She's in good general health, but an illness like
this should be watched. I'm relieved you're going
to be here,' he added. 'That maid of hers will
only do what Miss Lorrimer says.'

Which must mean he wanted a strong hand for
Maud, so Josey made sure she remained in bed
until the doctor said she could get up. On Maud's
first night downstairs, Josey decorated the tree,
which Theodore had put up that day. Brian
stopped by unexpectedly and she used his help in
putting ornaments and lights on the top
branches.

Before he left, he asked her to the Christmas
dance to be given Saturday night at the club his
parents belonged to. She agreed to go if Maud
was well enough.

'Then I guess I'll have to stop by Wednesday
and make sure Miss Lorrimer is better,' he
suggested smilingly.

'Just how serious are you about that young
man?' Maud asked as they were eating their
lunch on Saturday.

She had a right to wonder, for Brian had popped
up nearly every day that week, usually with a small
gift for her and a matching gift for Josey. She had
watched him closely and saw he was falling in love.
She wondered if Josey was aware of it.

'I'm not serious at all,' Josey smiled at her reassuringly, digging into her grapefruit which had been sprinkled with ginger. 'We're just friends—you know that. He *is* nice, though.'

'Oh, *nice!*' Maud shrugged. 'Nice is dull. What you need is a man who can make you realise your full potential as a warm, sensuous woman.'

Josey burst out laughing. 'Is that a quote from one of your books?'

Maud tilted her small nose. 'You need a love affair, Josey Smith! And not with Brian—even if he is love with you. You've maintained a hands-off policy so long with men that you've wrapped yourself in cast iron. Brian is a case in point. He's safe, so you continue to see him, but do you think you're being fair?' Josey looked startled and Maud seized her opportunity. 'You need to fall in love with someone exciting, romantic. Someone like Thorne for instance.'

'Funny, I thought all you were interested in was getting rid of Eve Sanders,' Josey said dryly.

'Oh, that!' Maud waved her hand airily. 'I always intended for you and Thorne to fall in love. Not in the beginning. I wanted to keep you apart then. But, after John died, I knew it was the right time. I consulted Zelda, and she agreed that the stars, the time, the date are all propitious.'

'I wish I'd never given you my birthday,' mumbled Josey.

'You can't argue with Fate, my child,' Maud said grandly. 'And it *is* Fate! Why, I felt the intensity in the air when you met Thorne, and I was only a bystander. If you remember, you turned pale. Now, that was from a drop in your blood level . . .'

'Maud, you have one heck of an imagination!'

Josey scoffed. 'My blood level didn't drop. I was pale because I'd just played a fast game of tennis. You're no doctor, Maud, so stop trying to pretend you know what you're talking about.'

'The air between you crackled with awareness!'

'It crackled with dislike—and that's a direct quote from your latest book! And incidentally, everything your precious nephew has done so far has confirmed you were right to keep us apart!'

Maud smirked. 'Hatred is the other side of the coin of love, my dear. Your horoscope says you will go through a turbulent period before your stars join. You are an Aquarius, and he's a Taurus, so naturally, the combination is volatile. There's really nothing you can do to stop it, Josey.'

Josey leaned her chin in her palm and regarded Maud with exasperated affection. Maud, that crazy optimist, was never going to change, but there were times when she could be extremely aggravating. 'Forget it, Maud!' she said emphatically. 'I'm not going to become Thorne Macallan's mistress simply to satisfy you and Zelda Kaminsky.'

Maud's eyes widened. 'His mistress? Josey, dear, I'm talking about marriage!'

'And that is the funniest thing I've heard yet. He told me he had no intention of ever marrying.'

'Indeed?' Maud looked thoughtful. 'Then, you've already . . .'

'I've already got the treatment,' she said grimly. 'Forget it, Maud. I'm not a character in one of your books and I refuse to allow you to go stepping in and out of my life.'

'But, Josey, when Thorne said that, he didn't know . . .'

Josey leaned forward and patted the fragile little hand. 'Look, love,' she explained gently. 'You know me. I'm the marrying kind of girl. I've never had a love affair—I'm even, God forbid, a virgin. When I was nineteen, I had a bad experience—a real bummer that put me off men forever. And Thorne is the last man I'd want to get involved with. You said yourself you thought it best to keep us apart. Nothing has changed. We're still the same people, and I couldn't take the pain if I got hurt.'

'Josey, you've got to be willing to take a chance in life.'

'Darling, I despise the man.'

'You're fascinated by him.'

Josey started to deny it, then paused. 'Yes. But he's hard.'

'You could soften him.'

'Not that man. Drop it, Maud.'

'No, I can't do that, without trying to explain about Thorne. Perhaps, if you know him, you'll understand. I blame myself for what happened, for not having more control over my younger sister. Our parents were dead, and I had always indulged her, spoiled her; then, as I saw the way she treated other people, I realised Dinah was a bitch, a greedy, amoral, selfish little wanton. God forbid me, I was relieved when she married Jordan Macallan. He had money—which Di craved—and he was older, and I thought capable of controlling her. Instead, the day of the wedding, she offered him a cold-blooded bargain. Her freedom and a generous settlement for a son.' Josey gasped. 'She left two weeks after

Thorne was born and never saw him again, nor even tried to. Twenty years and three husbands later, she died in a car accident in France. She was with her latest lover. I was notified—none of her so-called friends knew she had a son.'

Josey pitied Thorne. She thought of her own mother, dying also in a car accident, but leaving behind a legacy of beautiful memories to comfort her grieving daughter.

'Unfortunately, Jordan did not spare the boy. He grew up knowing exactly what his mother was—her bargain with his father. He wasn't left with even a dream to cling to. Hating women as he did, Jordan would not have any but male servants in his house. Everyone told me what a cold household it was; what a lonely little boy Thorne was. When he was about fourteen, I met him through some—er—mutual friends, and after that, we saw what we could of each other.'

'Did his father find out?'

'Eventually,' Maud said dryly, 'but he allowed it when he saw I was harmless. You see, he really loved his son—he taught him what he did to keep him from being hurt, as he was. Unfortunately, he had loved Diana.'

Josey gave a sharp gasp.

'Yes, that was the tragedy—and why he was so bitter. Thorne grew up to be a handsome devil. Jordan spoiled him, of course, and besides that, his looks got him any woman he wanted. It amused Jordan to watch his son become an accomplished heartbreaker. Fortunately Thorne had a good brain and a talent for hard work. When he graduated from law school, his father expected him to join his firm, but Thorne wanted to try it on his own. It was the first time he had ever crossed Jordan and he flew in a rage and threatened to disinherit him. There was a girl— Thorne's latest—who took it seriously and being particularly mercenary, she dumped him. I don't think Thorne cared a fig for her, but so far as he was concerned, it proved his father had been right all along. When the woman tried to get him back, later, after he and Jordan were reconciled, Thorne was brutal in his rejection. His public humiliation of her was rather cruel.'

Josey shivered. Yes, he would be cruel. In none of their encounters, had he ever been kind. He had begun by accusing her of fraud and a form of prostitution, then made love to her with contempt. She ached with compassion for him after hearing Maud's story, but she knew she would be a fool if she let it make a difference. She couldn't try to comfort him—it would be like snuggling up to a man-eating tiger. She would be savaged to death.

The truth was that Thorne had the power to make her scream with pain. She didn't face the reason for it—it was enough to recognise the fact. For the sake of her future contentment, she had to stay out of his way. If she could.

CHAPTER EIGHT

THAT night, as she dressed for the Christmas dance, Josey's mind turned reluctantly to a subject it had been avoiding since her talk with Maud. Brian. Was Maud right? Was he falling in love with her? And was she subconsciously catering to his idealised picture of her without any real expectation of fulfilling his hopes? If so, she was wrong. She was using him as a buffer, and God knows, she knew what it felt like to be used. Brian was too nice to be hurt.

She looked at the dress she intended to wear. It was in a delicate shade of pink with tiny cap sleeves, a floating skirt and a modest neckline. Exactly the kind of dress to make Brian start hearing wedding bells.

She hung it back in her closet and started pulling hangers rapidly until she found what she was looking for. This dress should put paid forever to Brian's vision of her as his virgin bride. It was the one she had bought in Charleston.

Her tan was honey gold against the creamy white and her hair poured like molten copper down her back. She applied gold dust shadow to her lids and glossy copper to her lips, then stepped into a pair of high-heeled sandals. The dress slid over her head with a sinuous rustle. It was going to scare Brian to death, but it should open his eyes to her unsuitability. A woman wearing a dress like this looked like a woman available to a man with the right price—and that wasn't Brian.

Maud's eyes opened wide then lit with an inner amusement. 'Beautiful dress, darling,' she drawled. 'It should separate the men from the boys. Brian's here,' she added, raising her voice.

'What about a drink, Brian?' she asked solicitously, as she followed Josey into the living room.

He swallowed convulsively, his eyes mesmerised by Josey. 'I don't think we have time, Miss Lorrimer,' he mumbled. 'We've got to pick up Mom and Dad.'

'Oh, are your parents going with you?' Maud asked innocently.

'Yes, they look forward to this Christmas dance. It's one of the biggest nights of the year at the club. Old time band music, that sort of thing.'

'How marvellous. I like a boy who does things with his parents. Don't you, Josey?' she asked blandly.

Josey threw her a warning frown and held out her silky shawl to Brian. 'Is this dress too— much—Brian?' she asked gently. 'I'll change it if you like.' She felt a surge of affection for the boyish young giant.

'No, no, of course not!' he said quickly, then added gallantly, 'I'll be the envy of all the men.'

'Oh, I don't think there's any doubt of that,' Maud twinkled.

He thew her a startled, half-scared look and Josey leaned forward and kissed the wrinkled cheek. 'Behave yourself!' she admonished under her breath. 'I'm taking your advice.'

The dance was geared to the club's senior citizens, who were well represented. The music was reminiscent of that played in the thirties and forties—golden oldies. Josey and Brian sat at the table with his parents and their other guests and Brian's mother carefully avoided looking too often at Josey's naked back and shoulders. Even so, she was friendly. But, she would not have got on with Maud, who would have thought her a bore.

When Josey got up to dance with Brian, he held her gingerly, avoiding touching her back. Josey scared him tonight. He was wary of the sensation she was making, the attention they were receiving from the older woman. And their husbands, who all wanted to dance with Josey. The Marsden's table was the most popular one in the room.

During one of the band breaks, she and Brian left their table and threaded their way through the crowd to the bar. They were in the doorway of the small, intimately lighted room when they were stopped by what was, to Josey, an all too familiar voice.

'Hello, darling, miss me?' A hand slid around her waist and Thorne pulled her to him with a warning jerk.

Her face mirrored her shock. She looked up and met the narrowed glitter of angry eyes. He was expecting her to protest and instinctively, she knew he was prepared to make a scene if she did. In fact, she suspected he would even enjoy a scene.

'Hello, Thorne,' she said calmly. 'It's nice to see you're back. I wasn't sure you would come back, but Maud will be glad, I know,' she added politely.

Having firmly established the casual nature of their relationship, she waited with a feeling of impending doom as Thorne's face hardened into a cold mask.

'But surely you knew I'd come back for you, my sweet?' His ironical drawl held a tinge of appreciation for her tactics. 'I thought I settled all that the night before I left.'

Josey swallowed and darted a quick look at Brian. He was frozen with shock. By now, Thorne's hand was explicitly caressing her bare back and sliding suggestively beneath the loose folds at her waist. Every nerve in her body was jangling, but she couldn't shrug him off—his glittering eyes told her just what he would do if she tried it. So she was forced to pretend that she hadn't noticed his movements or the lazy mockery of his smile.

'I don't believe you two have met.' Josey was speaking between her teeth, meeting Thorne's amused look with a bright defiance. She performed the introductions rigidly, screamingly aware of the hand sliding down her spine. And he knew, damn him! He knew the effect he was having on her senses.

Desperately, Josey turned to Thorne. 'Did you bring a date? Brian, shall we ask them to join us?'

She saw at once that was a mistake. Thorne's eyes flared and there was a savagery in the hands that tightened painfully on her waist.

'You're a little devil, aren't you?' he said gently, his warm breath fanning her face. 'You know you're my girl.' He turned to Brian. 'I hope she's just trying to make me jealous, Marsden, because if I find out that anyone has been fooling around with my woman, I'll grind him right down to the ground.' He sounded friendly but his eyes were warning the other man off.

'I—I d-didn't know anything about t-this . . .' Brian stammered.

'You big bully!' Josey snapped furiously. 'You're a liar! How dare you imply we're l-lovers? Don't listen to him, Brian!'

Thorne turned to the other man. 'If you'll excuse us, Marsden, I'll take Josey home now. She's growing a little testy and her memory is failing. You noticed how she stammered over that word "lovers"? She always does that when she's lying.'

Brian gaped at both of them helplessly.

'I'll show you who's testy, you arrogant bully!'

'Would you like to continue our discussion at home where we can have some privacy?' Thorne asked smoothly, reminding her of where they were.

Josey looked around with a start. The bar was crowded and they had attracted a share of the attention, although their voices had been kept low. Brian was crimson with embarrassment.

Josey caved in. Thorne, she knew, was perfectly willing to go on just as they were, but she knew she was only humiliating Brian, who was apparently not willing to do battle for her.

'Brian, dear,' she said sweetly. 'Will you make my excuses to your parents? Apparently, Thorne has something he wishes to discuss with me in private.'

'So long, Marsden,' Thorne drawled. 'I hope I won't have to put you straight again about Josey.'

As they waited at the cloakroom for his coat and her shawl, he said admiringly, 'I like that dress, beauty. But from now on, I don't want you dressing like that for anyone but me. Understand?'

She glared at him. 'You despicable coward!' she blazed. 'I will *never* dress for you!'

He grinned. 'Does that mean you will undress for me? Oh, no, you don't!' He caught her wrist. 'You're not sneaking away to hide yourself in the powder room. Right now, you're so furious I don't trust you. You need your feathers smoothed.' His amusement deepened. 'Why the indignation? Surely you expected me tonight?'

'Why should I?' she demanded in a goaded voice as she stalked out of the club towards the car park.

He smiled slowly. 'Good old Maud. She knows all about the element of surprise. According to her, you've been burning the candle at both ends with Brian Marsden while I've been gone.'

Josey blinked. Good old Maud, indeed! 'Well, if I have, it's no business of yours!'

'Which is what we've got to get straightened out tonight.'

By this time, they had reached the car and he slid behind the wheel after seeing her in and carefully locking the door. 'We'll drive along the beach. There's no privacy at Maud's house and I have a lot to say to you.'

She shrugged. She was too hungry for him to be frightened. And hadn't he said that he had no intention of making love to her anywhere but in a bed? 'I can't stop you,' she said blandly, her anger already dissipating.

'No, you can't, can you?' he agreed smoothly, as he put the car into gear.

He pulled her to him as soon as he stopped the car, his mouth reaching for hers hungrily. They kissed as though famished, and when he raised his head, she was gasping for breath.

'I haven't been able to think of anything but you for a week,' he muttered, smothering her face with little, short kisses.

Passion flared between them like a lighted brush fire, rocking them out of control. All thoughts of fighting him off vanished in the rush of pure delight that sang through her body. They clung together, trembling, exchanging greedy, famished kisses, and when he raised his head, she brought it down to her mouth again. He fumbled at the neckline of her gown and she was frantic to help him, taking his hand and placing it on her naked breast, quivering with delight as he stroked it with slow, sensuous movements. With shaking hands, she unbuttoned his shirt, savouring the feel of the warm, damp flesh beneath her palms. She found the flat, male nipples on his chest and they hardened beneath her probing fingers.

He shuddered and she looked up quickly, her eyes gleaming beneath her heavy lids. His face had tautened to a mask of raw hunger, and she realised he was as aroused as she was. Her blood sang with triumph and she began to cover his chest with a series of small, warm kisses.

He caught her hands and held her away, then pulled her upright, into the circle of his arms.

'No, don't try to move. We've got to talk, darling. God!' He gave a low, shaky laugh. 'You go to my head, beauty.' He took a deep breath. 'Maud is going to have to get herself another secretary, I'll start working on it right away. But until I find someone, she'll have to make out with the nurse she had while she was in the hospital. She can type and Maud liked her.'

Josey listened in stunned silence. 'What are you talking about?' she asked dazedly.

'You're going back to Atlanta with me, when I go home after Christmas. I don't see how I can wait until then, but you're right, I can't seduce you under Maud's roof. I'll have to rent a suite at the hotel—we'll go there when we get frustrated. Like tonight.' He groaned. 'I can't wait any longer to have you in my bed. I'll call Maud, make some excuse.'

She began to pull frantically at her dress, trying to cover herself. 'Are you crazy?' she demanded. 'I'm not going to a hotel with you tonight or any other night. You know, you're unbelievable!' Her humiliation goaded her into angry, impetuous words. 'You storm into the club, break up my date with Brian, then tell me I'm giving up my job and leaving town! I haven't agreed to that!'

'But you will.' He smiled sharply, the bite of anger in his voice. He took her face between his palms and raised it to his. 'You know I can persuade you. In about one minute. That's all it will take.'

Her face flamed. 'Maybe you can—in this car! But there's no way I'm going to accompany you to a hotel, wait while you sign the register and then go tamely to a room so you can seduce me! By that time, I'll have snapped out of this mind-boggling orbit you put me into and I will flatly refuse to go! And this time, *I* won't mind making a scene before the hotel clerk or anyone else who is around! And the next day, I'll leave and you'll never see me again. That's a promise!'

He leaned back, eyes half-closed, listening while she talked. Now, he surveyed her thoughtfully. Apparently, her words convinced him, for when she finished, he said briskly, 'Very well, my stubborn little shrew, when do you want to leave here and live with me in Atlanta? And I do mean *live* with me. I want you there when I go to bed at night and when I wake up in the morning. And, incidentally, I've never said that to another woman.'

'Is that supposed to be an enticement?' she enquired coolly.

'I had hoped it might be. That and—oh, jewels, furs, a car. I'm willing to buy you anything—within reason, that is—for the exclusive use of your body for a specified length of time.'

She stared at him, astonished, and then, as his meaning sank in, she realised she was more hurt than angered.

'Whatever gave you the idea I was for sale?' she asked icily.

'Most women are,' he said drily.

'Perhaps most of the women you know are, but *I* am not! You know,' she went on bitterly, 'you take the cake as the most cold-blooded bastard I've ever known. Is that your answer to everything? Money? My God, but you are beyond belief!'

'I've never known a woman who couldn't be bought—with one sort of bribe or the other. Some just come a little higher.' There was a tinge of insolence in the hard, cold voice that made a cold chill run down Josey's back.

'Did it ever occur to you that your little circle of friends include some female barracudas?' she enquired hotly.

He shrugged. 'I gather from all this that you've set your price rather high? I should have known, from that experience on the beach.' He laughed harshly.

'Indeed I have!' she said sweetly. 'My price is marriage.'

She was surprised that he answered her seriously. 'I don't believe in marriage—for me, that is.'

'Sorry! That's my price. Nothing less!' she quipped fiercely. She looked at him with contempt. 'No one's twisting your arm to marry me, you know.' She rubbed her bare arms beneath her shawl and shivered slightly. A corrosive sense of disillusionment was eroding her spirits, making her feel cold and desolate. 'Will you please take me home,' she added numbly. 'I'm cold.'

He started the motor and turned up the heater until a blast of warm air poured out of the vents. Josey held out her hands to the welcome heat. She wondered how long he was going to sit there without moving. Probably not until he made another attempt to make her change her mind. To sell herself. She rubbed her arms tiredly. She didn't think she could take much more of this. She was aching all over with the sort of pain that shouldn't belong to a woman who had just proudly refused to live in sin. She should feel good, but she hurt.

He put the car in forward gear and made a U-turn, then he stopped again and sat with his hands on the wheel, the motor idling.

'Marriage, you said? How soon?' His voice was clipped, unemotional. 'Shall we get the licence Monday?'

She gasped. 'Do you mean—are you asking me to marry you?'

'That's what you wanted.' He looked at her coolly. 'As a matter of fact, things may work out better this way.'

'Now, wait a minute!' she protested weakly. 'I—I never said . . .'

'But you did, my dear,' he corrected her mildly. 'I have accepted your terms. I will marry you. I shall take a great deal of pleasure in telling Brian Marsden to get out of your life,' he added brutally. 'He's lucky I didn't push his damned face in.'

'You mean—you *cared*?' she asked blankly. 'You were *jealous*?'

'Like hell,' he replied harshly. 'Surely you're experienced enough to recognise that? For God's sake, did you think you were the only one who was carried away?' He sounded almost bitter, as though Fate had played a dirty trick on him. 'You have me climbing the walls, my dear. I'm willing to sacrifice a great deal to get you—even my freedom—but let me warn you now, don't play me false. Marriage will give me the exclusive right to your body and I expect you to remember that and all the other clichés. such as "Till death do us part". I'm not going into this thing expecting a quick divorce at the end. Eventually, I shall want children—so remember that, too. Or I shall make you sorry you were ever born, my beautiful little wife to be.' He put the car into gear and added grimly, 'Now, let's go home.'

Naturally, Josey slept poorly that night. Exhausted by the emotional ups and downs of the evening, terrified by the necessity of making a firm decision, she tossed and turned until nearly dawn.

On the way home, she tried to talk to Thorne only to have him refuse to discuss the matter until they reached the house. By that time, she was shivering with tension and he reached into the back seat and came up with a heavy, fleece-lined car coat.

'Here, put this on. You're in shock. It was

sleeting today when I left Atlanta,' he added, by way of explanation for the coat.

'Look, Thorne.' Her teeth were chattering as she huddled in the thick, luxurious coat, warming her with the scents from his body. 'Let's have an end to this thing. You can't want to marry me just because I won't become your mistress. It— it's crazy! We don't even like each other!'

He listened impassively, his stern face clearly defined in the moonlight. When she came to an uncertain halt, he said, 'How about if we signed a marriage contract, setting forth the terms just as though it was a contract? Would that suit you?'

'Oh, God,' she said wearily, resting her head against the back of the seat. 'You don't even understand what I'm talking about.'

'You're tired.' His voice was almost kindly. 'Go upstairs and sleep on it. Think about what I can offer you. And, Josey, remember, I'm aware of all the objections as well as you, and I still think we can have a good marriage. You'll see it all clearly in the morning.'

Josey stumbled to her room like a sleepwalker. She stripped off her white dress and put on a nightgown. *Tired?* She was exhausted! There was no thinking over anything, either—she knew her answer now. She couldn't marry Thorne Macallan. Vividly, that day in the courtroom came back at her. He had looked at her only once—when she started screaming at him—and his face had been cruel with distaste. She had hated him; the memory of that hatred was still with her. Did she want to marry that man? A man who had proposed merely because he couldn't get her any other way? Who had said nothing about love, tenderness, respect—but a great deal about unrequited lust. Who had actually had the nerve to mention children—*children!*—in a marriage like that!

Of course, if the tables were turned and she was the kind of greedy, unprincipled character he thought she was, she'd marry him just for revenge. And it would be a fine one, when he learned she was an ex-convict. He would deserve it, too, for he had made a normal life impossible for her. How could she marry any man without telling him of her past first, and perhaps run the risk of losing him? She toyed with the idea of telling Thorne who she was immediately after the ceremony. She could imagine his fury when he learned she had kept the truth from him. No— she hadn't that kind of courage, she thought bleakly, remembering the cold rage that could turn that handsome face into a pitiless mask. It might be a perfect revenge but she would do her share of paying. Besides, she acknowledged drearily, she wasn't that kind of person. She couldn't do it to any man, not even Thorne Macallan.

Every time she reached this point, Josey's emotions took over and she was hit by such a wave of depression she wanted to curl up and die. Oh, God! She buried her head in her pillow, twisting and turning, fighting the treacherous memories of his lovemaking. Pain shafted through her body, bringing an involuntary moan to her lips. She wanted him! She ached for him. She had been so confident that she wouldn't fall in love, yet instinct had told her all along that Thorne Macallan would eventually bring her pain. Why hadn't she listened to that voice? Although, by then, it was already too late. By

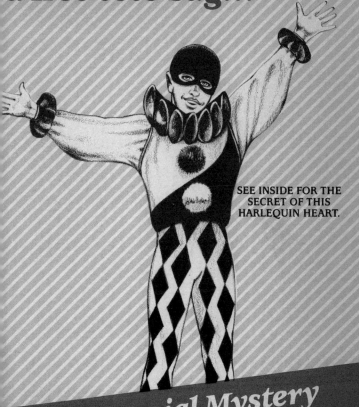

Get 4 free books...
a free tote bag...

SEE INSIDE FOR THE
SECRET OF THIS
HARLEQUIN HEART.

. plus a special Mystery
Gift when you give your
heart to Harlequin.

⋖ IT'S A ⋗
HARLEQUIN HONEYMOON
A SWEETHEART
OF A FREE OFFER!

4 NEW "HARLEQUIN PRESENTS"–FREE! Take a "Harlequin Honeymoon" with four exciting romances—yours FREE from Harlequin Reader Service! Each of these hot-off-the-presses novels brings you all the passion and tenderness of today's greatest love stories…your free passports to bright new worlds of love and foreign adventure!

But wait…there's <u>even more</u> to this great <u>free offer</u>…

HARLEQUIN TOTE BAG–FREE! Carry away your favorite romances in your elegant canvas Tote Bag. At a spacious 13 square inches, there'll be lots of room for shopping, sewing and exercise gear, too! With a snap-top and double handles, your Tote Bag is valued at $6.99—but it's yours free with this offer!

SPECIAL EXTRAS–FREE! You'll get our free monthly newsletter, packed with news on your favorite writers, upcoming books, and more. Four times a year, you'll receive our members' magazine, Harlequin Romance Digest!

<u>Best of all, you'll periodically receive our special-edition Harlequin Bestsellers,"</u> yours to <u>preview for ten days without charge!</u>

MONEY-SAVING HOME DELIVERY! Join Harlequin Reader Service and enjoy the <u>convenience</u> of previewing eight new books every month, delivered right to your home. Each book is yours for only $1.75—<u>20¢ less per book</u> than what you pay in stores! Great savings plus total convenience add up to a sweetheart of a deal for y<u>ou!</u>

START YOUR HARLEQUIN HONEYMOON TODAY– JUST COMPLETE, DETACH & MAIL YOUR FREE OFFER CARD!

HARLEQUIN READER SERVICE

❧ FREE OFFER CARD ❧

PLACE HEART STICKER HERE

FREE TOTE BAG

FREE HOME DELIVERY

4 FREE BOOKS

PLUS AN EXTRA BONUS "MYSTERY GIFT"!

☐ **YES!** Please send me my four HARLEQUIN PRESENTS ® books, <u>free</u>, along with my free Tote Bag and Mystery Gift! Then send me eight new HARLEQUIN PRESENTS books every month, as they come off the presses, and bill me at just $1.75 per book (20¢ less than retail), with no extra charges for shipping and handling. If I am not completely satisfied, I may return a shipment and cancel at any time. <u>The free books, Tote Bag and Mystery Gift remain mine to keep!</u>

108 CIP CAJT

FIRST NAME_____LAST NAME_____
(PLEASE PRINT)

ADDRESS_____APT._____

CITY_____

PROV./STATE_____POSTAL CODE/ZIP_____

PRINTED IN U.S.A.

*Offer limited to one per household and not valid for present Harlequin Presents subscribers. Prices subject to change.

Affix special Heart on reply card to receive your Mystery Gift!

BUSINESS REPLY CARD

FIRST CLASS   PERMIT NO. 70   TEMPE, AZ

POSTAGE WILL BE PAID BY ADDRESSEE

Harlequin Reader Service
2504 West Southern Avenue
Tempe, AZ 85282

NO POSTAGE
NECESSARY
IF MAILED
IN THE
UNITED STATES

then, he had already awakened those turbulent emotions that were lashing her now.

The next morning, she felt like the dead. Shadows lay like bruises under her eyes, and her head was pounding. She had an unpleasant interview ahead with Thorne and right now, she felt like she'd burst into tears the first time he spoke to her.

She dragged herself downstairs to find that Thorne hadn't waited for her consent. In his typical high-handed manner, he had taken matters out of her hands and told Maud that they were engaged. Josey was caught by surprise, then too stunned to contradict him. By that time, Maud's congratulations were ringing in her ears, Maud's joyful face, damp with tears of happiness, smiling at her. She couldn't—it was literally impossible—to say it wasn't true. He had counted on that, of course, the devious bastard. She glared at him over Maud's shoulder, mouthing the words 'I want to talk to you.'

'You'll have to excuse us for a minute, Maud,' he said blandly, meeting Josey's glare with an amused smile. 'I think Josey wants to be private with me. Shall we go into the library, my dear?'

She turned on him in a fury the instant the door closed behind them.

'How dare you put me on the spot like that?' she stormed. 'You knew I couldn't tell her the truth after seeing her like that!'

'Of course I knew it,' he said calmly. 'Tell me, Josey, if I hadn't forced the issue, what would you have told me this morning?'

She said nothing, her face speaking for itself.

'I thought so. I was right then, to take it out of your hands.'

She glared at him. 'It would serve you right if I *did* marry you,' she burst out sullenly.

He smiled ironically. 'Why not?' he drawled. 'You say you hate me. Why not marry me, my sulky little termagent, and make me sorry for every dirty trick I ever played on you?'

All right, she thought stormily, you deserve everything you're going to get! When you find out the truth about me, we'll see how you like it then! But she wanted to fling herself into his arms and bawl. She had no idea that her face was reflecting her conflicting emotions, until he pulled her into his arms in an abrupt gesture of sympathy.

'Don't worry, beauty,' he murmured, 'we're going to make it.' A fleeting smile crossed his face, dry with irony but oddly gentle. 'We already know we want each other on the most basic level. Believe me, the other will follow. I promise you, it's going to be a good marriage.'

Perhaps if she had been given time to think, she might have backed out anyway, but Thorne didn't give her time. They were married three days later, the day after Christmas, in Maud's living room with her old friend, Judge Pendleton, performing the ceremony. Annie and Theodore were their only witnesses.

Christmas Day had been spent quietly, with just the three of them enjoying the Christmas dinner. The red candles and the Christmas centrepiece added a festive note to the table, which was set with Christmas china. Maud's face was triumphant as she raised her glass in a toast to their future happiness, and Josey saw that it was most definitely her day. Thorne had given his aunt a diamond and sapphire brooch, in the shape of a lark on the wing, and Josey had piled a number of small gifts under the tree for her— her favourite perfume, an amethyst bonsai tree, a book she had been wanting to read . . .

Josey had shopped for Thorne's gift at the last minute, and fortunately found something she thought he might like. For the man who had everything, she had bought a framed painting— an original—at one of the little art shops on the island. The price was high enough to meet the mental price tag in her mind. It was a seascape done by a local artist, and Thorne seemed pleased with it.

Of course, it could not meet the cost of the fur coat he gave her, or the flawless topaz ring surrounded by diamonds, that he said matched her eyes. She wore it on her right hand, for her wedding ring was to be a plain wide gold band.

She had made up her mind. When the time came for their eventual parting—and it would— she would walk out with nothing but the wedding band. He had called her greedy and mercenary once, and she suspected he still thought that was her real motive in marrying him. She intended to show him she wanted nothing of his, not even the seascape she had chosen for him.

CHAPTER NINE

TWELVE hours after their quiet wedding, Josey stood on the dazzling white sand of a Caribbean beach, and gazed out at the glittering blue ocean. The beach was private, a half-moon sickle of sand protected on both sides by an outcropping of rock which stretched out to sea. It gave them their own small, private bay.

Behind her was the house, a big white villa with deep green awnings and a trellised terrace that was dappled with morning sunlight. The house belonged to friends of Thorne's, and had been lent to them, complete with servants, for their honeymoon. The arrangements had been made without Josey's knowledge.

She had been too tired last night to fully appreciate the beauty of the house and grounds. They had arrived late, after midnight, after a delay at the Miami airport, and Josey had fallen exhaustedly to sleep before Thorne came to bed.

The sound of the closing door awakened her and she sat up quickly, disorientated for a moment. She leaped out of bed and dressed hurriedly in her bikini, then picking up a towel, left by way of the sliding patio door. As she reached the beach, she saw Thorne strike the water and start swimming strongly out to sea.

She watched his head in the water and felt wretched. The realisation had come to her in the night: she had been wrong—so wrong!—to marry him. She had been as despicable in her behaviour as he had ever been. Worse—for she had condemned him to more than a two-year sentence: she had sentenced him to life with a woman who had a prison record. A woman he could never respect. Of course, she would be leaving when he learned the truth, but he had made it clear his idea of marriage was a commitment for life. She was bound to leave scars, even on his hard shell of indifference. She slumped to the sand, white-faced. She was going to have to tell him the truth while the marriage could still be annulled. And the thought was like having a sentence of death.

Suddenly, she sat up and looked out to sea, her eyes fearful. There was no sign of Thorne. She stood up and stared, but the bay was empty. Nervously, she looked over her shoulder towards the house. George, the elderly manservant, was placidly setting the table for her breakfast. She saw the glint of silver as he shifted the coffee pot. Running towards the terrace, she came to a panting stop before George.

'Will you eat now, madam?'

'I'll wait on my husband.'

'Oh, he had his breakfast early this morning before he went for a swim.'

Oh, God, she thought desperately, doesn't he know about the danger of cramp? She wet her lips nervously. 'I don't see any sign of him. Do you?'

George looked up and casually surveyed the empty bay. 'I expect he's behind those rocks.' He poured her orange juice and pushed the coffee pot forward. 'I have hot croissants, madam . . .'

'I don't want anything right now,' she said abruptly, and ran back towards the shoreline.

There she paced, her eyes roaming frantically over the bay, the outcropping of rocks, even the edge of the water. There was no sign of him. She tried to reassure herself that he was a good swimmer; he knew what he was doing; but she was growing more panicky by the second. Her heart was pounding and her mouth grew dry with terror.

Soon, she was crying, as she wrung her hands and paced the beach. Dimly, she comprehended that her reaction was not normal—that she hadn't been herself for days. She had been depressed and weepy and reacting jumpily for a week or more—long before her marriage. And she knew why. She was in love with Thorne Macallan. Perhaps she had always been in love with him. Certainly, her subconscious had recognised it as early as that first day at Maud's. She had watched him avidly, eager for signs that her words were hurting him. And once they had kissed, she had recognised she was dangerously attracted although, and here she had been a stupid nitwit, she had told herself she was immune. All right to lie to Maud, but she had been a fool to lie to herself! A fool to imagine she was marrying for revenge.

Her eyes searched the water again and she had already advanced into the sea as far as her knees, when she saw his head bobbing on a wave. He lifted an arm and waved, and she saw that he was carrying snorkeling equipment. She felt foolish and limp with reaction. Turning, she ran back to the towel she had dropped on the sand, and scooped up her sunglasses. She was going to have to pull herself together before he got back.

By the time he strode out of the water, his suit

and flashing smile the only white against the dark tanned skin, she was stretched out on her towel, her arms down beside her, her eyes hidden by the sunglasses. He stood over her, the water running down in glistening rivulets among the hair on his legs and chest.

'Very nice,' he said, his eyes gleaming with sensuous appreciation.

She took off her sunglasses and looked at him in simulated surprise. 'Hello. Enjoy your swim?'

'Very much. Had your breakfast yet?'

'No, I thought I might swim first.'

'I'll take you snorkeling, if you like.'

'Later. I've never done it before.' Her hands trembled as she fumbled with her bottle of suntan lotion.

'Roll over and I'll do your back.' He dropped to a crouch beside her.

'No, you—that's all right,' she said hurriedly.

He didn't bother to answer. Taking the bottle from her, he leaned forward and unclipped the back of her bra with one quick movement. She gasped and caught the dangling scrap of cloth as it fell from her breasts.

'Don't!' she cried jerkily, glancing at the terrace. It was empty.

'Don't worry. George and Edie won't see us. You couldn't get them out of the air conditioning unless it was an emergency. Anyway, didn't you know people are going bra-less on the beaches round here?'

He grinned at the expression on her face as she lowered herself gingerly to her stomach. He began to smooth the oil over her shoulders and back with long, sweeping movements. As she had known it would, her flesh reacted with an involuntary shiver. He ignored the tell-tale giveaway, and continued to stroke her skin with slow, unhurried movements. His hands covered her ribs, spanning her slim waistline and finding the soft, flattened edges of her breasts. He fumbled with the ties of her bikini pants, ignoring her spasmodic movements of protest, and began a kneading action at the base of her spine. Just as she thought she couldn't stand anymore of the delicious torment, his hands dropped lower, to her legs and calves.

His hands were weaving an erotic pattern on her flesh. Wherever he touched, her body responded with a tingle of desire until her skin was sensitised to the point of torture. When he reached her inner thighs, she gave a low groan and he slid his hands beneath her waist and turned her over.

Her eyelids opened slowly, feeling as though they were weighted. She was staring into the face of a stranger, his cheekbones heated by a flush, his pale eyes darkened with hunger. They travelled slowly over the length of her body, seeing the signs of her desire in the restless movements; the taut nipples. Leaning forward, blotting out the sunlight, he lifted her into his arms and began to move, half-running towards the house.

'The servants . . .' she gasped.

'To hell with the servants!' he muttered thickly. 'They're paid to make themselves scarce at a time like this!'

Josey blushed at the thought of the staid elderly couple seeing her carried, naked, in the arms of a husband who obviously was intent on ravishment.

In the bedroom, Thorne put her down and began to strip off his swimming shorts. He was impatient, his arousal evident, and he was not allowing her time for maidenly modesty or objections.

She was staring at him fixedly when he looked up and noticed her. 'What's the matter?' he asked impatiently. Apparently, he read something of her expression for his lip curled. 'Don't try to pretend you're seeing anything you haven't seen before! Get on the bed!'

'Thorne, I—I think I'd better tell you something I—s-should have told you before . . .!' she began helplessly.

'*Now?*' He looked incredulous.

'You've got to know before we go any further——'

'Damn you to hell, you cheating little bitch, I already know all I need to about you! Don't you go cold on me now!'

He gripped her shoulders with cruel, merciless hands and flung her brutally on the bed, sending her sprawling backwards among the sheets. Her flame-tipped hair spilled across the pillow and she stared at him in helpless panic, trying to form words that would stop him long enough for him to listen to the rest. Her hands pushed weakly at his chest, as he half-fell across her body, and he thought she was trying to deny him. An ugly expression of cruel, ruthless passion darkened his eyes, and he stopped her mouth with his, his tongue forcing the unuttered words back in her throat.

Then, with a muttered oath, he thrust her thighs apart with brutal, rough hands, and drove harshly for his own satisfaction. The pain ripped her apart, and she gave a low, muffled cry. She felt his hesitation, his pause, but he did not stop. She lay beneath him unmoving and listened to his deep, hoarse breaths, as he gasped out his pleasure into the softness of her throat. Finally, he subsided with a long, racking shudder, and she listened as his heart gradually slowed its pounding and resumed a normal beat. He raised himself on his elbows and stared into her white face.

His eyes were smoky with disbelief and something that might have been pain. 'My God, Josey, why didn't you tell me?'

She threw him a look of bitter contempt, then rolled to the other side of the bed, where she curled in a tight ball. 'Go away.'

He touched her tentatively, and she shook off his hand. 'Leave me alone.'

He gripped her by the shoulder and dragged her around to face him. 'No, you don't,' he said in a hard voice. 'I'm not having a sulky bride. I could have made it easier on you if I'd known—it didn't have to be that way. You didn't tell me you were a virgin. Why?'

'Would you have believed me?'

He knew what she meant. 'Not at first, no, but you could have tried. And after we were married . . . Damn it, Josey, you were acting like a cold-blooded little tease! I thought you were playing that little game of yours.'

'What game?'

There was a long pause. His face was withdrawn, remote. 'You're the one with secrets. How the hell would I know if you don't tell me?' He waited a moment, then said mildly, 'What about John? I thought . . .'

She whirled on him with flashing eyes. 'I know, you thought I was his mistress because two horrid old miserly women told you so! You didn't bother to ask John's lawyer or old Maggie Anderson about the annuity I bought her! No! You *thought* I was guilty!' she blazed.

'I'm sorry, Josey,' he said gently. 'Why didn't you set me straight?'

'Because I was angry. You had prejudged me, just as you've done since the first day you ever saw me!'

His eyes narrowed alertly. 'What do you mean?'

She faltered and stopped. Tears rolled down her cheeks. 'I want a divorce. This marriage isn't going to work. I mean it, Thorne. I want you to take me back to Atlanta and start a divorce right away.'

He laughed, a low, rollicking laugh that was filled with such tender amusement that her heart contracted with agony. 'Ah, Josey, you're just disillusioned. Your first experience with passion has proved a great disappointment, and you've decided to chuck it all and run, like the habitual little coward that you are! You're not running away from this, my darling, and you're certainly not backing out on our bargain. No, beauty, you're staying and seeing this one through.'

She stared at him stonily, willing her face to remain unmoved. 'I want a divorce.'

His eyes darkened. 'You're not getting it,' he said evenly. 'At the risk of repeating myself. You're merely scared and irrational.'

'I was never more rational in my life.'

'Perhaps you're nursing another secret, locked away in that squirrely little brain of yours?' he suggested blandly. 'If so, get it out, Josey. You'll feel better for having told it.'

She drew a sharp breath. He was getting close, too close. 'The only secret I have,' she said nastily, 'is an all-consuming dislike for you! After what has just happened, I can't go through with it. You make my flesh crawl!'

His hands tightened spasmodically on her shoulders, his face hardening with a vicious look of anger that reminded her that he had a fierce temper and the strength to go with it. For a moment, she was frightened as he brought his anger under control. 'You're mine,' he said deliberately. A sardonic amusement coloured his voice as he stared into her apprehensive eyes. 'Yes, you're right to be scared. If I believed you, I might kill you, but I know you're lying for some purpose of your own. But that's not important so long as you understand that you are my wife. I bought and paid for you, you double-crossing little cheat, and you're keeping your side of the bargain if I have to tie you to my bed. You wanted the luxuries my money can buy, and you wanted sex, and that's *all* you asked for out of this marriage. So far, I've lavished a good supply of the first on you, and I'm prepared to follow through with the latter, whether you fight me or not. Right now, incidentally, because I think you need another lesson in who you belong to.'

He leaned over her. In spite of the brutality of his words, his eyes were warm with a trace of compassion and a dry smile flitted around his mouth. He placed a hand softly on her breast and deliberately, began to arouse her. She knew she couldn't fight him, but she lay with clenched fists, obstinately glaring at him.

He glanced up, his eyes smoky with amusement. 'I think you do me less than justice, my sweet,' he taunted silkily. 'Do you really think this doesn't tell its own story?'

He flicked the taut peaks of her breasts, then lowered his mouth to the soft mounds. He wooed her with soft, gentle movements, tormenting and teasing until she was gasping and twisting restlessly beneath his hands. The dark tide of desire was running strong and Josey, loving him as she did, was helpless to control its flow.

At the peak of her pleasure, she sobbed his name and gripped his shoulder, her nails digging into the flesh.

'Gently, darling, gently,' he murmured against her throat.

Finally, she lay quietly in his arms, her breasts rising and falling with her breathing. He watched her with heavy lidded eyes and when she looked at him, he smiled.

'I think we'll try a shower now. I'm covered with salt water and you, my little sensualist, are covered with the dew of love.'

'The dew of love?'

He ran a lazy hand across her face and upper lip. 'See?'

Slipping off the bed, he lifted her into his arms and carried her to the bathroom. There, he turned on the shower and put her in it, then stepped in with her. His grin flashed at her startled look.

'We have to share,' he said wickedly. 'There's a water shortage.'

Palming a bar of soap in his hand, he lathered her luxuriously while her body answered with tingling shivers. Then, he shampooed her hair, bracing her against the flat planes of his stomach while he soaped and massaged her scalp. His hand moved through the strands, separating them for the flow of rinse water, and he kissed her frequently on her upturned face. When he finished, he quickly scrubbed himself, then towelled them both dry.

He tucked his towel around his lean hips and followed her into the bedroom, where he had her sit on the side of the bed while he towelled her hair dry. When he finished, he parted the long strands of burnished copper and sought her mouth with soft, sensuous lips.

'What about it, Josey. Going to accept my apology?'

'Apology?'

'For prejudging you. I made a hell of a mistake, and I'll regret it the rest of my life. I won't do it again. But, Josey, from now on, trust me.' He sounded stern but his eyes were kind. 'You haven't, you know, not once so far. You don't even know how. How can we make a marriage without trust?'

'How can we make a marriage without love?'

He re-arranged the coils of hair so they no longer covered her breasts. 'We have something better than love,' he replied, leaning forward to kiss the soft, tender flesh. 'A lot of marriages don't have as much.'

She understood what he meant. But her love had governed her strong, physical response to him—she knew that, even if he didn't. 'Is it enough?' she asked hesitantly.

'It's enough,' he said positively. 'Don't trust love. Trust this.' He caressed her wrist, picking up the increased heartbeat beneath his long, lean fingers.

Her mouth opened to receive his gentle kiss. She couldn't have left him, anyway, not unless he sent her away. Not now. And she couldn't tell him the truth, either, for the same reason. She was in love and she was afraid of losing him.

CHAPTER TEN

THEY stayed a week at the white house on the beach before returning to Atlanta. Thorne taught Josey to snorkel and they spent many hours underwater in the little curving bay. Their days followed a pattern—the mornings were spent swimming, boating, fishing ... Then, the long languorous siesta, spent behind drawn drapes and closed doors in their bedroom. After that, a lazy cocktail hour was followed by an excellent meal cooked and served by George and his wife, Edie. They had the house to themselves after dinner. The servants did not live in, but returned to their own home at night.

Occasionally, they went out to one of the hotels to dance, but mostly, they stayed at home, playing cards, dancing or merely listening to music before returning to the bed that was the scene of their greatest pleasure. It was an idyllic existence and Josey dreaded to see it come to an end. She knew things would inevitably change when it did.

She found it easy to talk to Thorne here, resting in the shelter of his arms on the sofa, while they listened to music—the haunting strains of Ravel's *Bolero* or the Bach which Thorne's methodical mind preferred.

He asked questions about her childhood, and she told him about her parents and Medlar's Mill. He wanted to know every small detail, and for the first time, she found it easy to talk about them. The raw pain she was used to feeling was gone.

But when she came to the part about her decision to leave home and go to Atlanta, she proceeded more slowly, choosing her words with care. She shrugged aside most of his questions.

'It was too silly, to think I could sing professionally,' she said off-handedly. 'I soon found I couldn't compete in that sort of world.'

He did not talk about his own childhood. A wall went up when she tried to talk about it, and she, knowing all too well that memories can be painful, didn't try to probe.

It was only when they made love that she forgot herself. At night and every dawn when the cool morning breeze awakened them, they would turn to each other as though famished. She never got enough of him. Tentatively at first, then with more confidence as he welcomed it, she began to initiate some of the caresses. He called her a sensualist, but she could see that he was pleased by her responses. And so long as he was pleased, he wouldn't look elsewhere, she reminded herself.

They returned to Atlanta to find the city in the middle of its worst winter storm in years. It was locked in ice, shivering under the impact of snow and sleet from the north. On the way from the airport, Josey's body, accustomed to the tropical temperatures, shivered in the fur coat.

'Poor darling. Are you cold?' Thorne hugged her protectively, but he sounded absent-minded. He was back home and already, his mind was on other things. Josey, watching him, shivered again and wondered if this could be the beginning of a change.

'Do you like it?' Thorne watched her closely as he showed her over his penthouse apartment. It was on the top floor of a highrise dwelling in a fashionable section of Atlanta, and Josey learned as they rode up the elevator that Thorne owned the building.

She did not answer. Thorne's apartment was nothing like John's shabby home or even the luxurious comfort of Maud's. It was—Josey searched for the word—impersonal. It lacked warmth, although everywhere she looked she saw paintings and art objects.

'If you don't like it, you may change it.'

Josey started, and realised it was important to him for her to like his home. 'Don't be absurd! I wouldn't dare—it's too beautiful.'

He shrugged. 'I brought in a decorating firm and gave them a free hand. The only thing I asked was that they find a place for my paintings.'

Josey had already noticed the paintings. They were placed at strategic points on the walls, a collection of early artwork by American artists, mostly from the nineteenth century.

'My father began it and after he died, I added to it,' Thorne told her.

Josey, in the time-honoured fashion of knowing what she liked, not what was art, thought some of it hideous while others appealed. She knew the collection must be valuable, for she recognised several of the names. When she thought of her cheap little seascape, she wondered how Thorne had felt when he saw he might be expected to hang it.

'Come on.' He pulled her forward, a hand loosely clasping her wrist. 'I want you to meet Wragge and then you can help me with something.'

Sam Wragge was a very dignified elderly man who reminded her of Theodore. He bowed his head gravely in response to Thorne's introduction but she felt that he was withholding judgment on her until he knew her better.

'If you have a problem, go to Wragge,' Thorne told her. 'He hires the cook, buys the food, and supervises the cleaning. *And* sees to it that no one touches the papers on my desk. Is there anything else you do, Wragge?'

'I hope I do what needs to be done to the best of my ability, Mr Thorne,' Wragge replied with immense dignity.

'Oh, yes, I forgot. He's known me all my life and doesn't think I'm a bit funny,' Thorne added with a grin.

Making a mental note never to touch Thorne's papers, Josey gave Wragge a straight look. 'I hope we can be good friends.'

Wragge merely bowed his head and Josey was left with the distinct feeling that he wasn't really sure.

Back in their bedroom, Thorne brought out the painting which she had given him for Christmas. It had been packed away in the bottom of his suitcase. 'Now, where shall I hang it? I thought it might do in here . . .'

She flushed, looking around the room desperately. Dominated by Thorne's king-size bed which was covered by a sweep of chocolate velvet, the luxurious white carpet and white walls provided a natural background for a Harrison painting—a scene of rural Georgia. On another wall was a pair of portraits, apparently of Thorne's great-grandparents, going by the style of clothes. The woman had Thorne's eyes. From here, the artist appeared to be Sargeant. Josey was distressed. A fortune in paintings on his walls, and he was going to hang the one she had given him!

'Thorne, please don't,' she blurted impulsively. 'I won't be offended, I promise you, if you don't hang it.'

He stared. 'What are you talking about?'

'You can't hang it in your apartment, among these others!' she protested. 'Give it away, throw it in the garbage, but don't hang it here. It's—cheap!'

'What does that matter? You gave it to me.'

She smiled at him gratefully. 'That's very sweet of you, but why don't you let me get rid of that thing for you?'

'Damn it, Josey, you're obsessed with money, aren't you? So what if it cost a fraction of what the other paintings are worth? Do you think that's all that matters to me? Do you have so little trust in me you think I'd discard your gift that—that callously?' he added angrily. 'You don't give me much credit, do you?'

Josey flew at him. 'Darling, put it where you like! I was wrong!' She pulled his head down and kissed him frantically. '*Please* hang it! Here! Or over there!' She babbled until he laughed and pulled her into his arms.

So they made it up but it was their first quarrel and signalled the beginning of others. Their little spats—for that was what they were—seemed to flare up over nothing and so far as Josey was concerned, all seemed to originate with Thorne. They centred on two themes: money and trust. His belief that she married him for his money and that it was all she needed to make her happy. It

was so far from the truth that Josey did not know
how to fight it, except to hope that he would
eventually realise it for himself. Her own guilty
conscience made her sometimes wonder if she
read more into his occasional sardonic references
to her lack of trust than was there. She could, of
course, have proved her trust by confessing to her
past and the impulse that made her marry him for
revenge, but she knew she couldn't do it without
losing him, and she wasn't ready yet to face that
possibility.

He knew, of course, that she hadn't loved
him when she married him, so he was free to
assume it was because of his money. She hadn't
been frank about her past, although he had
given her plenty of opportunities, so he knew
she was withholding her trust. She couldn't
even tell him she loved him, for once she
opened that Pandora's box, all of her secrets
would come out, including the most terrible
secret of them all.

She sometimes wondered why he had married
her. Oh, he had wanted her, she knew that, but
now that she was more knowledgeable about sex,
she wryly admitted he could have broken down
her resistance and made her his slave, just as she
was now. She was responsive, passionate, and
they were sexually compatible. Would she have
held out against an all-out attack? She didn't
think so. And he must have known all along what
strong weapons he had—a man with his expertise
would always know it.

So why did he? She was merely another girl,
another face in the crowd. A beautiful face, yes—
but then, so were the others. What made her so
special that she had caught the gold ring on the

merry-go-round? If she could only find out why, she could keep on doing it, or keep on being it and hopefully, keep him.

After racking her brain, she finally came to the conclusion that it was because he knew another woman—Eve, for instance—would have expected more, demanded more, of his time and attention. And, she was left alone a lot. He worked long, hard hours, and when he came home, he did not need a demanding wife. What he needed was what he got—an acquiescent wife who studied his moods and adapted herself to them, a willing slave, a lover . . .

Oh, he was kind, but sometimes she thought his kindness was the impersonal sort of a busy parent who lavished money instead of attention on a child. He bought her a car, a little Skylark that she adored. He opened charge accounts for her in all the major stores, and a current account for small, personal expenses that he kept topped when it fell below the original mark. She was able to shop where once she had merely wistfully looked.

Like any woman, she found it fun, of course. The first day she was informed her accounts had cleared, she went on a binge. Since most of her clothes were resort things, she bought lavishly. The doorman had to help her clear out the car and into the elevator, and she piled the packages high on the bed to surprise Thorne.

'Show me,' he drawled, lounging on the bed and watching her excited face as she tossed the beautiful garments about. A slight smile touched his lips as he settled himself against the pillows.

'I'll model them for you,' she said eagerly, and retired to the bathroom.

He watched with lazy amusement as she came

out in each outfit, twirling and posturing like a model. She kept the best for the last, a sheer nightgown she had bought with exactly this moment in mind.

'Like it?' she asked archly, twirling before him.

He sat up, a gleam of anticipation in the pale eyes as he pulled her into his arms.

'Smart girl,' he murmured later, as they lay entwined in each other's arms on the bed. The nightgown was draped across the bed post, and he glanced at it with a trace of sardonic appreciation. 'To wear it last, I mean. It paid for all the rest. Sure you weren't afraid to let me see the bill until you had sugar-coated the pill?'

She laughed uncertainly, sensing the underlying cynicism in his words. Is this what his other girls had done? Had she acted like a mistress instead of a wife? 'Didn't you like my floor show?' she asked hesitantly.

'Umm.' His face was lying on her breast, his tongue lazily teasing the nipple until it tautened in his mouth. 'Just keep on the way you're going and I'll have no complaints.'

She could take that two ways, but she felt the sting of his cynicism whenever he gave her anything. He was always bringing home something for her—a piece of jewellery, an item of lingerie, a fine leather purse—sometimes a book. She didn't know if he sent his secretary to shop for him, or if he did it himself, but she always took his gifts as a sign that he thought of her during the day.

When she tried to thank him, he would look at her with that familiar glint in his eyes.

'You know how to thank me,' he would drawl, and the taut hunger in his face would send shivers of anticipation down her spine.

She knew he had been conditioned since boyhood to believe that this sort of cold-blooded barter system was a marriage, and she did not know how to break through his shell of cynicism. He had erected it to avoid being hurt and it had hardened over the years. And always, there was the painful possibility that this was the way he really wanted it.

Wragge was still wary of her, although he did not seem to resent the idea of having to account to a woman rather than Thorne. He showed her over the flat, how the burglar alarm system worked, where the linens were kept, the sets of china, Waterford crystal and heavy antique silver cutlery with the Macallan initial engraved on its handles. He gave her a rundown on the servants' working hours. The cook, who was excellent, came in every day, of course; the cleaning woman, three times a week; and a cleaning service took care of the heavier duties, such as carpets and curtains.

But the cook and the cleaning service continued to report to Wragge; the house ran like a well-oiled machine, and there wasn't much for Josey to do. If she had had a home instead of an apartment, she could have found pleasure in gardening. Once, Thorne had mentioned his old home, 'a barn of a place', but he hadn't offered to show it to her. She didn't think he had any intention of moving from this conveniently located apartment—unless there were children.

Josey shivered at that thought. Thorne wanted children, of course—he had said so—but her own feelings on that subject were mixed. Perhaps she had shown him in some subtle way how she felt, for he hadn't mentioned it again. She loved children, longed for one with all her heart, but she wondered what would happen if he ever found out about her past. Would he take the child—if there was one—away from her? She could be shown to be an unfit mother. She would never give up her child. Josey hugged her stomach protectively. Not that she was pregnant—she had only been married a month!—but if it happened, what would she do?

She stood at the window, and looked down on the skyline of Atlanta, and it seemed as though all the weight of the world was on her shoulders. She should be happy—she had everything a woman could want—but so long as she lied to Thorne, she would find it difficult to live with herself. And what a mean, sordid motive it was, marrying for revenge! She could never explain it without earning his contempt.

Wragge, walking in just then, was struck by the desolate droop of her shoulders. He cleared his throat tentatively, and when she looked around, the offer of coffee he was about to make was dropped, and instead, he asked if she would like to help him wash the crystal.

She smiled, and he decided he liked that look. It wasn't pushy, and she was obviously pleased to be asked. He liked that, too.

'Sarie,' he said, meaning the cleaning woman, 'is heavy-handed, so I always do the fine dishes and crystal myself.'

Later, his hands in soapy water, he struggled to make his position clear.

'Ordinarily, I wouldn't need help——'

'I love to help you.'

'It's this dinner party,' he lumbered on.

'What dinner party?'

He looked surprised. 'The one you and Mr Thorne are giving tomorrow night.'

'Oh, that dinner party.' She dropped her eyes to the goblet she was polishing.

'Do you have any special instructions about it?'

'I'm sure you know more about that sort of thing than I do, Wragge,' she said evenly, unwilling to let him know it was the first she had heard of it. 'Just carry on as you usually do.'

That night, Thorne mentioned it. 'It came up unexpectedly, when my cousin called. She and her husband will be in town overnight and they want to meet you.'

'I didn't know you had any relatives except Maud.'

He shrugged. 'Elaine is my father's cousin,' he said brusquely. 'She'll probably bring a wedding gift—she's the sentimental type,' he added drily, with a contempt that seemed to indicate dislike.

'I've asked two of my law partners and their wives, too, so we won't have to endure Elaine and Ralph's company on our own,' he added, reinforcing that impression. 'Do you have anyone you'd like to ask?'

Josey hesitated. Dr and Mrs Abernathy had been John's friends. He was a retired professor of mathematics, and she was a motherly sort who had always been kind to her. She gave their names reluctantly.

'I'll have Miss Pettigru send them a note. And perhaps—the Vinellis,' he added suddenly, in a speculative voice. 'Stephen and Zoë Vinelli might—er—provide a distraction.'

Once again, Josey wondered about his cousins whom he was obviously being forced to entertain. Or was it her whom he was uncertain of? She was uncomfortably aware of that possibility the night of the dinner party, while she was dressing. She chose a dress that was elegant, but understated. Suddenly, Thorne loomed up behind her in the mirror, and softly nuzzled her nape as he draped a slender gold chain strung with gold and jade beads around her neck. It nestled in the discreet cleavage of the dress.

'You look beautiful—and very hostess-y,' he added drily.

'I'm nervous.'

'Why? Your appearance and that hint of shyness will strike exactly the right note with Elaine,' he said impersonally. 'As a matter of fact, you're the most self-possessed woman I've ever known.'

Somehow, the double-edged compliment steeled her enough so that she had the courage to go and greet their first guests, Thorne's cousin, Elaine Jessup, and her husband, Ralph. She disliked them on sight. Elaine's face wore the petulant droop of a self-imposed martyr, and Ralph was bluff, hearty and smelled strongly of a mixture of alcohol and a floral after-shave lotion.

Elaine gave her a limp hand but Ralph, after one appreciative look, pulled her into his arms and gave her an enthusiastic kiss.

'So this is my new little cousin!' he boomed. 'Thorne, you're a lucky dog! I wish I'd seen her first, cousin!'

Josey recognised the type—an ageing ladies' man who automatically made a pass at anything in skirts. And when the female was young and personable, he could be counted on to make a second pass, and a third . . .

'You didn't tell me your wife was so beautiful, Thorne, although knowing you, I should have guessed it.' He squeezed Josey's waist, his taunt holding a hint of a sneer.

'Unless you need a prop, I suggest you let her go so she can greet the other guests,' Thorne said sardonically, giving Josey a hard look.

Ralph laughed again. 'Reluctantly, my dear boy! But don't go too far away, sweetheart. I want us to get better acquainted.'

Thorne gripped her by the hand and literally dragged her away from Ralph and out into the hallway.

'Do you suppose you could avoid encouraging him?' he asked coldly.

Josey was stunned. 'I—I was merely being friendly,' she faltered.

'Friendly I can do without. I don't want the evening ending with Elaine in a flood of tears,' he snapped unfairly.

The doorbell rang again and they had to answer it before Josey could make a reply. It was his partners, arriving together, with their wives. They were older men, and had been junior partners when his father headed the law firm. They were followed by the Abernathys.

Their arrival gave Josey the time she needed to pull herself together although she was already resigned to a disastrous evening. She left them to slip into the dining room and change the cards, putting Ralph beside the unknown Zoë Vinelli. It was a calculated risk, without knowing Mrs Vinelli, but she had no intention of warding off Ralph's roving hands throughout dinner.

She re-entered the hallway in time to see Thorne at the door, greeting the Vinellis, so she joined them. Stephen Vinelli was a short, stocky man with grizzled hair and a big, friendly face. He beamed at her with a kindly smile as he congratulated Thorne on marrying such a lovely young woman.

His wife was at least thirty years younger than her husband, a hard-faced redhead dressed in a couturier gown. As she greeted Josey, her eyes restlessly appraised her face, figure and clothes.

When she spoke, her speech was shockingly common.

'Where've you been hiding her out, Thorne?' she demanded in a nasal drawl that assaulted the ears. 'Everyone's been wondering if you intended to keep her hidden, pregnant and barefoot. After all, one month and no one's had so much as a glimpse of her.'

'They've been on their honeymoon, Zoë,' her husband reminded her with a hint of reproof in his voice.

'Oh, sure, and I bet Thorne hasn't been exactly wasting his time. But Mrs Macallan knows what I mean. I mean—a woman likes to be taken out and shown off occasionally, unless she's a dog.'

'Mrs Macallan, indeed!' Stephen laughed heartily. 'I intend to call her Josey and if she doesn't call me Stephen, I shall spank her!'

Josey smiled warmly. 'Stephen, then.'

'And I'm Zoë,' his wife drawled, tucking her arm under Thorne's elbow. 'And now that that's all taken care of, let's go in to the bar. I'm dying for a drink, Thorne, and you know what I like.'

Zoë did not waste any time on the older women in the room. She gave a comprehensive glance at the men, and her eyes settled on Ralph like a bee approaching honey. He, too, seemed to recognise a kindred spirit. In a matter of minutes, they were laughing and talking together. She was a perfect recipient for his broad type of sexual conversation. It did not seem to bother Stephen, who was deep in conversation with Thorne, but it reacted immediately on Elaine.

Josey, trying to talk to the other guests, grew increasingly uneasy about her. She began to see what Thorne had meant by 'floods of tears'. Elaine couldn't take her eyes off her husband and her face grew more doleful. Really, Josey thought exasperatedly, it was all Thorne's fault. He had been the one to bring this trio together. He knew Ralph's brand of humour—she didn't. Unless they were all such horrors, he had thought they'd cancel one another out. If so, he had been unsuccessful. Nothing could cancel out this miserable evening.

Zoë and Stephen stayed on after the others departed. Stephen and Thorne were deep in a business discussion and Zoë watched them, her hungry eyes fixed on Thorne in a look that was all-revealing.

'How does it feel to have married the city's most eligible bachelor?' she asked bitterly. Josey didn't answer, and she stood up abruptly. 'How about showing me the powder room?'

'I see you haven't made any changes to the place,' she remarked, pausing before one of the paintings with a covetous look on her face.

'No. I couldn't improve on perfection.'

'That's what Eve always said,' Zoë drawled.

'Eve?'

Zoë looked back over her shoulder at the entrance to the powder room. 'Oh, didn't I mention it? Eve Sanders is a great friend of mine. I must say, she's right about you.'

Josey followed her, braced for what she was sure was coming. 'Oh? In what way?'

'I expected a looker—Thorne always went in for

stunning women. Like Eve. He could take his pick. But you're the last one I'd expect him to pick.'

'Are you through?' Josey asked politely, holding open the door.

'Not quite.' Zoë leaned forward and touched up her lips with lipstick. 'I mean, you're a looker, all right, but you haven't got that extra—quality that someone like Eve has.'

'I'm sure you don't mean that as a compliment but I'm going to accept it as one,' Josey said blandly.

Zoë's hard blue eyes met hers in the mirror. 'See? That's what I mean! If I'd said that to Eve, she would have lost her temper. Thorne likes a woman to be exciting, sexy.' She ran her eyes over Josey's dress. 'You won't keep him, of course, but I guess you know that already. A lot of woman have tried, but he's . . .' she hesitated, searching for the right word.

'Fastidious?'

'Yeah, I guess you could say that. You probably think I have a personal axe to grind in this . . .'

'You shouldn't try to read my mind,' Josey said gently.

'I really like you,' Zoë added insincerely, 'but I'll give you a friendly warning—you'd better be careful around Eve.'

'How *kind* of you,' Josey drawled sarcastically.

Zoë's eyes were avid on Josey's pale face. 'She's out to uncover some dirt on you. Anything she can give to Thorne. She wants to break you two up. She knows you're hiding something about your past—she could tell you were nervous when she questioned you. And her father's a judge—she has access to court records.'

Josey had had a shock but she struggled to hide it from Zoë's greedy eyes. But not even for her pride's sake, would she stand here and listen to this a moment longer.

'You'll find everything you need in here,' she said evenly, and walked out.

When she returned to the living room, she saw Thorne studying her pale face thoughtfully. She tried to act normally although it was difficult. As a first attempt as a hostess, this party had been outstandingly unsuccessful, she thought bitterly. Suddenly, Thorne stood up and suggested brusquely to Stephen that they talk at his office. By that time, Zoë had returned languidly to the room and it was time to go, anyway.

'What did Zoë Vinelli say to you?' Thorne asked as soon as they left.

'Zoë?' she repeated vaguely, thinking fast. 'She was talking about Eve Sanders.'

'I can imagine,' he said contemptuously. 'What did she say?'

'They're great friends, you know.'

'No one is Zoë Vinelli's friend.'

Josey added bravely, 'They wondered what you saw in me.'

He looked amused. 'And did you tell her?'

'I wasn't sure I knew myself. She thinks it's only a matter of time before you're tired of me.'

'God!' he burst out cynically. 'The bitchiness of women when they get together. It never ceases to amaze me. All right, beauty, come upstairs with me. I'll show you what I see in you. Then, you can tell me if you think I'll get tired of you.'

Their coming together that night was wild and passionate—almost savage—and she thought she would die from the glory of it. Afterwards, they lay side by side, trying to get their breaths back.

His hand sought hers, and he raised the palm to his lips. 'Well, my darling, do you see why I won't get tired of you?' There was an undernote of laughter in his soft, caressing voice.

She said nothing, and with a contented little murmur, he pulled her into his arms. Later, his head pillowed on her breast, she lay awake for a long time, her eyes wet with tears. She knew now why Thorne had married her.

CHAPTER ELEVEN

ONE thing had been accomplished by Zoë Vinelli—she had made Josey determined not to be 'hidden' away any longer. Pregnant and barefoot, indeed! Josey hadn't missed the sidelong glance the other woman had cast at her waistline.

Josey knew from the size and shape of the envelopes that much of the mail that came to the apartment included social invitations, although Thorne probably received his share at the office or in phone calls. The mail was placed on his desk, where he usually pushed part of it aside unread. The morning after the dinner party, Josey went in to his desk and for the first time, investigated those unopened envelopes that bore the 'and Mrs' inscription. One that sounded promising was for a party the following weekend, and when she approached Thorne about it, he agreed to go after a quick sardonic look at the name of the hosts.

It was for one of those large cocktail parties where one goes to see and be seen, not for intelligent conversation and certainly not for a pleasant relaxed evening. On the way there, Thorne casually mentioned that the host was a client, then added that they had known each other since they were boys. He did not say anything about the hostess.

As soon as she saw the house, Josey knew that Thorne's old buddy had money. She was glad that she had chosen the dress she wore—a rustling jade green with a wide cummerbund of navy blue. With it, she wore the necklace Thorne had given her, matching jade earrings, and her diamond bracelet. This time, there was nothing understated about her appearance, or her dress.

'Are they millionaires?' she breathed, as they mounted the steps to the front door.

'Yes,' Thorne replied shortly. She was clinging to his arm, and he smiled at her. 'Relax. Millionaires don't bite, either.'

It was a beautiful house, but if she had thought Thorne's apartment cold and impersonal, this house multiplied that impression a dozen times over. The rooms were vast and beautifully furnished, a perfect background for all the beautiful people who were crowded in them. They were stopped many times by friends of Thorne's who wanted to meet her, but gradually, they were moving towards the back of the house, where the lesser crowd was.

When an elderly gentleman stopped Thorne to talk about a case, Josey listened for a while, then growing restless, accepted a glass of wine from a waiter passing with a tray. From where she stood, she could see a table filled with goodies, and finally, she was tempted to go and investigate.

She wandered around the table, holding her glass of wine, observing the food, then finally decided to choose a stuffed mushroom.

'I wouldn't, if I were you.'

He was standing beside her, watching with a lazy, relaxed smile. As good-looking as Thorne, he also had that easy air of assurance that distinguished Thorne, and made him so formidable. There was a glint of masculine appreciation in the eyes that were observing her. *Smooth!* though Josey ironically. But compared to Thorne, a lightweight.

'Why not?' She was holding the mushroom to her mouth.

'I have it on good authority that our hostess uses glue in her fillings.'

'What shall I do with it, then?' She gravely held out the offending mushroom.

'Give it to me.' He nonchalantly returned it to its tray. 'There. If you do it with aplomb, no one dares question you.'

'Will aplomb work if you've already bitten into it?' Her eyes danced.

The appreciative glint deepened as he gazed into their dancing golden lights. 'Ah! Then it is even more important that you let nothing faze you. You stare haughtily if anyone dares to look surprised until they begin to doubt what they've seen.' He grinned wickedly. 'Of course, it helps if you're the host.'

'Oh, are you the host?' Josey's face lit with a smile. 'Then, you're an old friend of Thorne's?'

'Yes. I saw you standing with him.'

'He told me he had known you since you were boys,' she added eagerly.

He smiled wryly at her eagerness. 'Yes, we were two rich motherless little boys. Does that make you feel sorry for me?'

'For him, perhaps, but not for you,' she reproved.

'Ah, I had hoped to gain your sympathy. Foiled again by my old chum! He always finds the most beautiful women first, then I have to take second choice. Where did he find you?'

Josey knew, of course, that he was married, but this was the sort of foolery that meant nothing, so she was still smiling as she explained, 'I met him through his aunt.'

'Maud?' He sounded surprised. 'That's a switch. Tell me, you don't mind sharing him?'

'Sharing him?'

'With your predecessor. The girl he's talking to now. Now, me,' he added persuasively, 'you won't have to share. I believe in being faithful to one girl at a time. How about it?' he smiled at her outrageously.

Josey turned and stared dumbly. The elderly man was gone and Thorne was deep in conversation with Eve Sanders. She watched with darkening eyes as Eve put her hand on his arm, and smiled cajolingly into his face. Her companion had been watching her closely, and now, he sighed dolefully.

'Ah, me, looks like I'll have to wait a while for my chance with you. You're hooked, aren't you? Her name is Eve Sanders,' he added, as Josey continued to stare at him blankly.

'I know.'

'And you mustn't trust her,' he continued smoothly. 'She's a real cool lady, and she doesn't accept defeat easily. Why not pay him back with some of his own medicine and leave the party with me?'

She stared. 'I couldn't do that! Are you crazy? Besides, it—you're the host! How could you leave?'

'Oh, I could, very easily, my dear. Do you have an arrangement with him?' he added abruptly.

'An arrangement?'

'Are you just a casual date, or living with him? But Thorne doesn't have live-in companions, so . . .'

'As a matter of fact, I do live with him,' Josey said demurely. 'So, I'm not really available.'

'So what? That won't stop him cheating on you. Look . . .' He stopped. 'I don't really know your name?'

'Her name is Josey Macallan, Jake, and don't you forget it.' Thorne slid a possessive arm around Josey's waist. 'She carries my brand on her.' He held up the hand wearing the wedding ring.

'Hell, old man, I didn't know you were married!'

'The hell you didn't—*old man*! Darling,' he added to Josey. 'I think you'd better display this more openly, especially when you are around someone as rapacious as Jake Lawton. Not that he'd let a little thing like a wedding ring stop him, but it might slow him down a little.'

Jake chuckled, his eyes gleaming with mischief. 'I never thought I'd see you take the plunge, buddy. Not an old bachelor like you. She's gorgeous and I'm smitten with her. Really,' he added, at the look on Thorne's face, 'I didn't know. I've been in California for weeks. When did it happen?'

'Last month.'

'Well, well. Just remember one thing—you'd better keep her happy, or I'll do my damndest to take her away from you.'

Thorne froze, his eyes a savage blaze. 'Perhaps you'd care to explain that?' he asked icily.

'I don't think so,' Jake said irresistibly. 'You might be tempted to take me outside and beat me, like you used to in the old days—er—Will you be going out for our usual golf foursome Sunday?'

'I sleep late these Sunday mornings.' Thorne's arrogant drawl was a blatant sexual statement made by one male animal to another. 'Let's go,' he added to Josey, rattling the chains of possession.

She looked at him stonily. 'I don't want to go now.'

'I don't give a damn what you want,' he said inflexibly, taking her arm with a firm grip.

As soon as they arrived home, she exploded with temper. 'Damn you, Thorne Macallan, I don't like the way you acted! Anyone would have thought I was a bone, the way you two were snarling over me! I didn't know who the wretched man was at first, until he——' She stopped abruptly.

'*Yes!* Until he told you he was your millionaire host, whereupon little bells—golden bells—started ringing in your head!'

'Are you trying to be insulting?' She was ominously quiet.

'I'm trying to be realistic!' he said bitingly. 'He made it clear he wanted you, didn't he?'

'I—yes—oh, I don't know.'

'He wanted you, all right. But don't take all the credit,' he added with insulting precision. 'He has a habit of wanting my women.'

She flinched. 'Yes,' she agreed coldly. 'I understand you two have the same tastes.'

'Why didn't you tell him you were married?'

'Because it was just fun—party fun—the kind I haven't had lately,' she reminded him bluntly.

'And won't again if you can't refrain from making dates as soon as my back is turned,' he said savagely.

'Surely you know me better than that, Thorne?' she asked wearily.

'I don't know you at all.' His hand went up to loosen his tie with a tired gesture. His face was exhausted, his eyes dark with disillusionment. 'You don't let me know you, Josey. Jake Lawton has one of those modern marriages, the kind I don't intend to have. Rachel Lawton is a very predatory female but he doesn't care how many men she takes to her bed or what she does, so long as she leaves him alone to play his own little games. It's true, he has been in California, and perhaps he didn't know I was married. But it wouldn't make any difference if he decided he wanted my wife. His friendship for me isn't that loyal. In fact, it would be a challenge.'

'I can't believe I'm hearing this,' she breathed. 'My God, Thorne, do you think it depends on *him*? I'm not available—to him or any man! Don't you trust me?' Her face was anguished.

'Do you trust me?' he asked quietly. 'Or am I merely the man who provides you with beautiful things for your body and the sex you crave?'

'I don't give a damn about *things*!' she sobbed. 'Take them all back! I don't want any of it.'

'Then you don't like the jewellery I gave you?' he taunted, pulling her into his arms and running a tentative hand across her throat, where the delicate little necklace lay. 'Rachel Lawton wears a diamond necklace worth a fortune around her neck.'

'I wouldn't want it, unless you went with it.' She put her arms around his neck and clung, beseechingly. 'Love me, Thorne. Let me prove to you that it's only you I want.'

'Why did you marry me, Josey?' he asked curiously, almost impersonally, as though her answer didn't matter. He held her loosely, his pale grey eyes probing her flushed face. 'It certainly wasn't because you loved me, was it?'

She avoided his eyes. 'You didn't love me, either.'

'I was honest with you. I wanted you most damnably. I still do. Was that it, Josey?' His eyes were bleak. 'I believe the appropriate word is lust?'

'That's all you want of me, isn't it?' she asked desolately, shivering a little.

'It's all I asked for, and I must admit, you've exceeded my wildest expectations,' he agreed quietly. His head swooped and his mouth found the little pulse that was throbbing wildly at the base of her throat. 'How does this pretty thing work?' he added thickly, his fingers fumbling with the cummerbund in the back of her dress. 'I wouldn't want to tear it.'

She showed him how it worked, and slowly, with consummate skill, he removed her clothes, then his own. She lay on the bed, looking at him, and flushed as she watched him observing her with the clinical detachment of a stranger. 'How beautiful you are,' he remarked unemotionally. 'Right now, that little pulse is going like a metronome.' He knelt beside the bed. 'I love to see it—it's a dead giveaway.'

'What does it tell you?' she whispered.

'That you want me,' he replied coolly. He put an idle hand and fingered the necklace.

'Oh, I forgot it!' She sat up and started to remove it.

'No, leave it.' He added derisively, 'It reminds me of my place in the scheme of things.'

She struck at him then but he caught her hand and bore it back to the bed. Then, he took her quickly, savagely, without preparation. To her everlasting shame, she met him with a passion that equalled his own.

'Are you hungry?' he asked afterwards, as they lay quietly on the bed.

'Yes. I'll cook something.' She half-rose.

'No, let me. There's sure to be something in the refrigerator. Poor darling,' he added consolingly. 'I should be the one to get the food as a penance. I meant to take you out to dinner after the party, but my bad temper got in the way.'

She watched smilingly as he returned with a bed-tray that was stacked with a tempting pile of corned beef on rye sandwiches with beer. She had propped herself on pillows, and he placed the tray betweeen them, then turned on the television set.

She had taken off her jewellery and she handed it to him.

'Put this on the dressing table for me, will you?'

He held it cupped in his palm for a moment, before putting it away, then crawled into bed beside her. 'You really don't care that much about the jewellery, do you?' he asked casually, watching her closely.

'I told you I didn't. Oh, I love wearing it—but *things* don't matter that much.' She shrugged. 'I guess it's the result of early training. My parents were poor, but we were happy.'

'Yes, I see,' he said slowly. 'I haven't been very nice about that, have I? I suppose I wanted to think that was the reason.'

'Wanted to think it? She frowned uncomprehendingly, hiding a flash of pain, then said politely, 'If it makes you happier, you may continue to think it.'

He looked at her oddly. 'I'm just beginning to understand that quirky sense of humour of yours, Josey. Forgive me, please?' He took her hand and turned it over, kissing the blue veins that threaded her wrist. Instantly, her pulse took off at a galloping rate, and he smiled slowly into her eyes. 'This is something that never lies, isn't it?'

'It can be very misleading,' she said gravely.

'Umm. Perhaps.' He picked up a spring onion and held it out to her, his grey eyes warm with laughter. 'Onions and pickles,' he said solemnly. 'So long as we both eat them, it doesn't count— so how about it?'

CHAPTER TWELVE

AFTER that, things went better until Josey came home one afternoon to find Thorne packing. She walked into the bedroom and saw that he was lifting shirts from the drawer to a suitcase that lay open on the bed. While she stared, dumbfounded, Wragge marched in with two suits in cleaners' bags. He took one look at her face, hung them quickly and left.

'Where are you going?' she demanded.

He looked up, his eyes narrowed thoughtfully. 'New York. On business. I'll be back in a few days—perhaps a week.' He grabbed up a handful of ties, looked at them appraisingly and chose three.

'You knew about this?' she muttered, dry mouthed. 'You must have known—you had Wragge send out your suits.'

'Don't make a fuss, Josey,' he said impatiently. 'I haven't time.'

'I'll take you to the airport,' she said quickly.

'Sorry, I prefer Wragge to take me. The car needs a lube job and he can drop it off on the way home.'

'Let me go to New York with you,' she said desperately.

'Are you crazy?' he asked incredulously. 'I'm running late as it is.'

'I can come on a later plane. What is the name of your hotel?'

'Sorry, Josey, but this is a business trip. I haven't time for you. That's exactly why I didn't tell you—I didn't want a scene.'

'I won't be a bother,' she promised humbly.

'Josey, much as I enjoy our sex life, I haven't the energy to supply your insatiable demands when I'm on a business trip like this one, working at the top level of my concentration.' Ignoring her stunned look, he added crisply. 'We've been retained by Stephen Vinelli to try to stave a takeover bid on his firm, and I'll need every bit of the staying power I have to fight the big business sharks.'

Josey felt as though she had been slapped. A rich tide of colour crept over her cheeks. 'I—I didn't mean . . . that wasn't the reason . . .' she stammered.

'Oh, come on, Josey,' he said ironically. 'You don't want me because you love me, but you *want* me.' He lifted his suitcase off the bed and hefted it in his hand. 'Don't you think I know that? You can barely wait until I come to bed at night before that sexy little body of yours heats up automatically. I know you were a virgin when I married you, but by God, obviously no one had tried very hard to turn you on before that!'

Ignoring her stunned gasp, he gave her a swift, hard kiss and walked deliberately out the door, leaving a shocked and humiliated Josey behind to try to pick up the pieces.

She lay on the bed, her eyes burning with unshed tears. Obviously, Thorne's desire for her was beginning to wane, and unreasonable as it seemed, her own desire was the reason. She buried her flushed face in the pillow, hot with shame. She was thankful now that he had gone. She was too vulnerable. She must never let him know how his cynical words had affected her. Somehow, before he got back, she was going to have to relearn how to love him by a whole new set of rules.

The trouble was that sex was meaningless when the man didn't love you. Oh, she'd be a fool to deny the physical pleasure—that was obvious— but the fact of the matter was that she loved Thorne, and he didn't love her, and the knowledge was eating into her soul like a canker.

Revenge! That old theory had been knocked for a loop long ago. Had she really thought she was marrying him for that? She knew now that it had never had anything to do with it. All along, there had been that deep, underlying attraction, that had begun in the courtroom when she was only nineteen, waiting to burst into full flower.

When she thought about a woman like Eve Sanders in his arms, jealousy tore at her like little claws. When she thought of his body, the smooth, supple muscles beneath the layer of polished skin, the power and strength of his body, she wanted to die of longing. The nails bit into her palms as her body tensed spasmodically, already aching for his touch. Could she really deny her desire, the way he made her feel? Could she play games with Thorne to keep his interest? It was getting increasingly hard to hide her feelings. There were times when she had to bite her tongue to prevent herself from giving them away. So what was she going to do when he returned?

Josey began to cry at that, stuffing a fist in her mouth as each fresh spasm of tears racked her body. She cried for herself, for the pain she was feeling and the pain she was going to feel when he didn't want her anymore. In vain, she tried to stop, telling herself that this was getting her nowhere, but these tears had been waiting too long to be dammed now.

Finally, after a long while, she fell into an exhausted sleep not awakening until Wragge startled her with a knock. The room was dark and cold. She lifted a sodden face from the pillow.

'What is it?' she called, in a voice that didn't sound like her own.

'It's Wragge, Mrs Macallan. Dinner is ready.'

She choked, then coughed. 'I—I'm sorry, Wragge, but I'm not hungry tonight.'

'Cook has prepared a special meal,' he said temptingly.

'Tell Cook I'm sorry. I really don't feel like eating.'

'Not even a cup of tea? Coffee?'

'Nothing.'

He went away then. Josey rose, moving stiffly like an old woman, and got into her warmest nightgown, then went back to bed. Without Thorne, the bed felt cold and comfortless, and she turned the electric blanket up, and hugged his pillow. The next morning, she crept downstairs at dawn, wearing her old warm bathrobe, a relic of her teen years. She hadn't slept much and her body ached as if she had 'flu. She needed a cup of coffee badly, and she sat, huddled in a kitchen chair, while she waited for the coffee to brew.

Wragge walked into the room, alerted by the smell of coffee. He looked slightly rumpled, but was dressed in his usual white jacket and tie. He stared at her slumped figure.

'I'm sorry to be messing up your kitchen,' she apologised. 'I didn't feel I could wait until you got up for some coffee.'

'It's your kitchen, Mrs Macallan,' he said

evenly, pouring her coffee. 'May I cook your breakfast for you?'

'Can you cook?' she asked, a ghost of a grin crossing her pale face.

'Well enough if I have to. I once did the cooking for Mr Thorne's father but then, he was a gentleman who liked plain dishes, not the complicated variety that Mr Thorne does.'

'You've known Mr Thorne a long time, haven't you?' Josey watched as he lifted a copper-bottomed pan from the hook and set bacon to grill.

'Since he was a little boy. He was always a quiet little boy, never dirty, never playing outside like most little boys. Hungry for a mother, I'd say. It filled a void in his life when he met his aunt.'

'Oh, do you know Maud?' Josey asked eagerly.

'You know her, too, then?' His eyes were intent.

'Of course. I've known her for years. I was working for her when Thorne and I met.'

'He didn't tell me that.' There was a curious look on Wragge's face. 'I thought you were one of his—er—ladies. You know—one he'd known before—er—before. Then, it follows you know Theodore?'

'Of course.'

'He's my brother.' Wragge smiled. 'He got the job with Miss Maud through Mrs Macallan—Mr Thorne's mother, that is. It was through us—my brother and me—that Mr Thorne first met Miss Maud. He was about fourteen at the time.'

Josey remembered Maud's words—that she had been united with Thorne through 'friends', but she had never expected it to be Wragge, or that he would presume to defy his employer.

'Was Mr Macallan angry with you?'

He smiled slightly. 'Yes, very much. But Mr Thorne stood up for me and finally talked him around. He soon saw Miss Maud was no threat to him. He was a jealous, possessive man, was Mr Macallan, and how he loved his son! What was his, was his, and he would have killed the first person who came between them. Mr Thorne is a lot like him,' he added, glancing at her.

Jealous? Possessive? Oh, yes, but not because of love, Josey thought painfully. Perhaps, the elder Mr Macallan's possessiveness did not stem from love, either.

'Was he kind to Thorne?' she asked.

'Oh, yes, spoiled him rotten. But Mr Thorne was good to his father—the only time he made him really angry was when he wouldn't go into his firm, after he graduated. After a while, the old man was proud of him. And the girls—they called here day and night.' Wragge deftly flipped an egg on to a plate of bacon and toast and slid it before her. 'Still do, so far as that goes, but he told me to answer the phone and tell them he was married. There have been a few who haven't let that stop them,' he mused, 'but he told me to tell 'em he lost all his money in the stock market.' He grinned faintly. 'That doesn't always stop them. Like that Mrs Sanders. She sure wants that man.'

'I know,' Josey said steadily.

He looked at her shrewdly, his eyes lingering on her pale face. 'She's no threat to you, Miss Josey, if you don't mind me saying so,' he said kindly. 'Mr Thorne's a one-woman man—like his father before him. He never married again, in spite of the way Miss Maud's sister behaved to him. A smart lady like you won't be put off by

Mr Thorne's hard manner. A smart lady will look beneath the surface.'

'Thanks, Wragge.' Josey smiled wanly. 'I know what you're trying to say, but it doesn't apply in my case. There's not much use in trying to soften a man who's simply not interested.'

'Not interested? In you?' Wragge smiled. 'I don't believe that, Miss Josey.'

Josey shrugged and Wragge wisely changed the subject. But their conversation had broken the ice—Wragge had accepted her. She was now 'Miss Josey'. They had long conversations through the following days—not just about Thorne, but on a variety of subjects. Wragge was a homespun philosopher, with a good judgment of human nature. And she was lonely, and loved to listen to his stories about Thorne when he was a boy. It filled the hungry void in her life.

Thorne called every night, at various times, and always asked to speak to her. He wanted to know every detail of her day, and she wondered if he suspected she might be seeing a man. She told him about her conversations with Wragge, and while she talked, a little of her loneliness crept in. Always, he ended by saying he was hurrying to finish, and would get back as soon as possible. But it was taking longer than the few days he had promised—it was going into a week since he had been gone.

One afternoon, towards the end of the week, Jake Lawton called her. In that lazy, amused voice that probably sent thrills of excitement racing down many a girl's spine, he asked her to have dinner with him. She refused, but he persisted, and finally, she ended by having to hang up the phone on him. Wragge was passing in the hallway just then, and she ended by telling him the whole story.

He chuckled even while he sympathised. 'Don't let Mr Jake get you upset. He's a rascally bandit. It's like a game he and Mr Thorne have been playing since they were young boys—trying to steal each other's girl. Mr Jake being married didn't slow him down one bit. His tricks never bothered Mr Thorne—he'd shrug and laugh because he never really cared if Mr Jake got the girl or not. That's because he never cared that much. But this time, Mr Jake's in for a shock if he catches him messing around with you.'

Josey smiled. Jake Lawton was altogether too charming for his own good. She wondered how many hearts he had broken. She couldn't help but like him, and suspected she could be his friend—in a strictly friendly way, of course—if Thorne ever got over this unreasonable jealousy.

Just then, the doorbell rang.

'I'll get it,' she offered, and Wragge returned to the kitchen, where he had been polishing silver.

She didn't look particularly neat, and hoped she'd be taken for a housemaid as she reached the door, wearing her old jeans with her hair screwed up in a bundle on top of her head. She flung open the door, a half-smile on her lips that gradually froze as she saw who the unexpected caller was. Tony Leyden's mouth dropped open. If she was shocked, he was stupefied. Her heart did a flip-flop.

'*Jocelyn!*' He gaped at her. 'Wha-at are you doing here?' He looked bewildered. 'Isn't this Mr Macallan's house?'

What awful luck, she was thinking desperately.

Why now, of all times, did she have to answer the door?

'Yes, it is,' she replied crisply. 'What do you want?'

She remained in the doorway, and made no sign of giving way to let him in. He was carrying a folder in his hand, and he looked confusedly from it to her, then back again.

'I—I was supposed to bring some papers—my boss said—some papers he wanted Mr Macallan to have when he got back from New York . . .' He stopped suddenly. 'Jocelyn, what are you doing here?'

'I live here, if that's any of your business,' she snapped.

'Live here?' He stared at her, open-mouthed, then an unpleasant expression crossed his face. 'Oh, I see.'

'I doubt it!' she commented icily. 'Are those the papers?'

'Yes.'

'Give them to me, then, and get out.' She slammed the door in his face.

But she was trembling and limp with relief at how narrowly she had escaped disaster. What if Thorne had been here? Far better that Tony should think her Thorne's mistress than his wife. He was capable of any sort of malicious mischief. She shivered, remembering the sly look on his face. To think that she had once allowed him to touch her, even kiss her! He no longer looked like an appealing little boy—a big weight gain had given him a self-indulgent, shifty-eyed look. Or had it always been there, and she had never seen it before?

An hour later, she was still shivering over the

memory of the encounter, when the phone rang. It was Tony.

'I think you left out something important while we were talking, Mrs Macallan,' he said, his voice filled with meaning.

Josey's heart began to beat faster and her mouth went dry. 'So what?' she asked contemptuously. 'I didn't jump to conclusions. You did.'

'I know, I know. But I've been wondering . . .' he paused, suspensefully. 'I went back to my boss and brought the subject around to the gorgeous red-headed chick who was living with Macallan now. He told me all about you. He was very enthusiastic about the new Mrs Macallan. Seems as though he and his wife met you the other night. Had dinner at your house.'

'So?' she asked coolly.

'You remember old Steve Vinelli, don't you? He has a young wife he needs to keep an eye on.' He snickered softly.

'And I'm sure you're happy to do it for him.' Josey's voice was loaded with contempt. 'All right, Tony, now that you've had your fun, get out of my life. I don't ever want to see you again.'

'I bet you don't, but let's discuss it over dinner tonight,' he said smoothly. 'Remember our old place—Luigi's?'

Josey slammed down the phone. She stood waiting, trembling, and less than a minute later, it rang again.

'Don't hang up until your hear me out.' This time, Tony was curt and businesslike. 'I gathered from talking to Vinelli that nothing was known about your stay in prison and I wondered if your husband recognised you? Dear Jocelyn. He only saw you briefly—and you were a blonde then. Or—if he did, perhaps he doesn't want it to be known around town that his wife is a jailbird? If you don't care who knows your story, stay home tonight. But if you don't want me telling everybody about you, starting with Zoë Vinelli, then be at Luigi's at seven o'clock tonight.' This time, he hung up.

He looked smugly satisfied when he saw her walk into Luigi's Italian restaurant that night. She hadn't changed—she was still wearing jeans and an old coat—and her face showed the strain of the last four hours.

'Sit down, darling.' He stood up and pushed out her chair. 'What shall it be? You used to enjoy Luigi's lasagna—remember? I see it's on the menu tonight...'

'Just coffee, please,' Josey told the hovering waitress. 'Look here, Tony,' she went on curtly as soon as they were alone. 'I have no intention of eating a meal with you. I am here for only one reason—to find out just what you meant by what you said this afternoon on the phone.'

'I was merely indulging my curiosity,' he said mockingly. The smooth, smug face wore an oily sneer. 'You know, you've really changed,' he added musingly. 'Even in those old jeans, you're more beautiful than you ever were—if that's possible. What did Macallan say when he saw you again? As I remember, you threatened to kill him—does he sleep well at night?' A pained expression crossed her face and Tony pounced triumphantly. 'He doesn't know, does he? I didn't think so—you've changed so much. He's the kind of arrogant bastard who'd have told it to his old buddy, Steve, and what Steve knows, Zoë

knows. And she didn't mention a word of it when
I asked her about you.'

'All right, Tony, so you've found out that my
husband doesn't know,' Josey said wearily. 'Do
you feel better?'

'As a matter of fact, I do. I'd love to be the one
to knock some of that arrogance out of his hide,
the pompous bastard! He's been riding for a fall
for a long time! But I'll forego the pleasure—
unless you force me to,' he added significantly.
Smug self-satisfaction was oozing from every
pore. 'Well, well, this *is* interesting! Now that
we've established who knows and who doesn't,
we can begin to talk business.'

'You conniving little sneak!' Josey said contemptuously. 'We are not talking anything!
You've been threatening me—now, it's my turn!
How would you like it if I told your boss that you
were a thief?'

Tony leaned back and laughed. 'Sorry,
Jocelyn, he already knows all about me. Oh,
didn't I tell you?' he added mockingly. 'Stephen
Vinelli is my godfather. He's an old friend of
my parents, and he's the one who got T. J.
Macallan to take my case. He wouldn't have
bothered, otherwise. There's not any way you
can hurt me with Steve Vinelli, except perhaps
get me fired. And I'm nothing but a glorified
messenger boy, anyway, so what's the difference?' He smiled broadly at the look on her face.
'Now, shall we talk?'

'What do you want, Tony,' she said tiredly.
'Money?'

He hesitated. Then, he shook his head. 'Sorry,
darling, but I have an ego to massage first.' When
she looked puzzled, he added, 'I want your body,

honey. You have grown into a very foxy-looking lady. You're no longer a frigid little virgin, and if I know T.J., he's taught you a few tricks that'll make up for all those times when I had to go home and take a cold shower.' He licked his lips reminiscently.

She had turned white and was staring at him in horror. 'I'll see you in hell first,' she whispered shakily.

His lips thinned into a cruel smile. 'Hell it will be, then, my sweet, for just as sure as God made little green apples, I intend to get some mileage out of this. If you don't put out for me, I'll go straight to one of those scandal sheets that specialise in muckraking and when I've finished telling everything I know—and a little more, too—your old man won't be able to hold up his face in this city again. And don't think they won't be interested, either, or you don't know what an important man your husband's getting to be. He's the leading force in that law firm of his, and the present political party is after him to run for office with an eye to eventually becoming governor.'

'How do I know you won't go to the papers, anyway?' she asked with desperate calm.

Her words seemed to indicate an acceptance of his terms, and his face brightened.

'Don't worry, I will keep my part of the bargain,' he said easily. 'But we'll discuss all that at our next meeting. Dinner, tomorrow night, at eight sharp. And this time, Jocelyn, wear something sexy. I like to be proud of my date.' His fingers brushed her cheeks lingeringly.

She shuddered and jerked away. 'I won't have dinner with you! What would I tell Thorne?'

'Nothing. You and I both know he's in New York until Saturday,' he said mockingly. 'After tomorrow night, we'll arrange our next meeting at a more convenient time.' The waitress arrived with his order just then and Josey used the diversion to rise, pushing her chair back with a loud scrape. 'I'll call and give you the place to meet me!' Tony called hastily after her retreating back.

Josey paid for her coffee at the cash register and walked out, her eyes dazed, her face white and anguished. The streets were dark, but she wandered aimlessly, too sunk in despair to notice where she was.

Just then, a taxi pulled up with a swish of wet tyres, and she realised it had been raining—she was soaking wet.

The taxi let her out before the entrance to the apartment hotel and the doorman gave her a big, beaming smile as he punched the elevator button to the penthouse. Fortunately, she was able to slip in without Wragge seeing her, and once in her room, she got quickly out of her wet clothes.

In her robe, she paced the floor, desperately trying to think. She had to come up with a solution before tomorrow night. Tony had given himself away several times—in his arrogance, he had forgotten that other people were not as stupid as he was. He had made it plain what his real plans were. He intended to make her his mistress—one payment would not be enough for him. She shuddered, thinking of those fat white hands crawling all over her body. Then, after he'd vented his bitterness and spite on her unwilling body, and drained her dry of all the money she could beg, borrow or steal from

Thorne, he would go to one of the scandal sheets and sell his story. His ego demanded that he ruin her for past imagined slights and snubs. She did not think he would try to blackmail Thorne—there had been a healthy fear in his voice when he spoken of him, in spite of his jeering attitude.

But, in the end, he would enjoy destroying them both.

She considered briefly telling Thorne the truth, but discarded the idea. That was no longer the issue, for he was going to learn the truth sooner or later. But *she* was the only one who could prevent Tony from selling his story to the papers. There was a slim chance that if she walked out and got a divorce, she could defuse the story by making it unimportant. An ex-wife was not nearly as newsworthy as a woman who aspired to be the governor's wife. If she let Tony know, he might not even bother trying to contact the papers, particularly if she was on her way out of town.

As a matter of fact, her accidental meeting with Tony had merely brought matters to a head a little sooner than she expected, for sooner or later, Thorne was going to find her out. And that meant a divorce. The signs were already there. He might even come back from this trip wanting a divorce. She caught her quivering lips between her teeth. She didn't want to have to see him again, so why not get out tomorrow and let him handle the whole thing?

Wragge tapped at the door.

'Miss Josey, are you all right?'

'Yes, thank you, Wragge.'

'Dinner is ready.'

Dinner? Dear God, she couldn't have swallowed a bite! She dragged herself to the door and opened it. His keen eyes swept her bleak face and disordered hair, still damp from the rain.

'I had—dinner out, Wragge.'

'I didn't know you had plans to dine out, Miss Josey,' he said gently, taking in her jeans and sweater, still damp, that had been flung on the floor.

'Oh.' She gulped. 'It was just an impulse. I went to a movie then stopped off at a pizza place on my way home.'

'Oh.' Wragge frowned worriedly. 'Mr Thorne called. He was disappointed to miss you.'

Josey's heart sank. Why couldn't she have talked to him just one more time, it asked despairingly. 'What did he say?'

'Nothing much. I told him I thought you got a phone call, then went out.'

'Yes, a friend called and asked me to meet her at the movies.'

Wragge went away reluctantly. He knew something was wrong but he couldn't put his finger on it. He was going to be a complication tomorrow if he saw she was leaving. He couldn't prevent her, of course, but he would try. And there was no way she could sneak past him, unless she chose her time carefully. Her thoughts whirled. About money—she was going to need some and she was determined not to use that put by Thorne into her bank account. She had a little of her own, left from her savings, in travellers' cheques.

She packed quickly, putting the resort clothes in one suitcase, her winter things in another. Most of her winter clothes had been bought by Thorne, but it would be stupid not to take them.

She would need them for a job. But she left her fur coat hanging in the closet and her jewellery in her dressing table, still in its velvet lined boxes. All but her wedding ring. She rubbed it against her cheek. She would keep it forever.

Suddenly, she was struck by a thought that almost felled her. This was going to mean the end of her friendship with Maud. Josey faced the thought, dry-eyed, filled with despair. For six years, Maud had been her best friend. Another hurt—could she weather it, too? She hoped Maud wouldn't blame her, but remember her with love, as she would do her.

CHAPTER THIRTEEN

THE next morning, she lifted the picture she had given Thorne down off the wall and took it to a gallery on Peachtree Street. To her surprise, they gave her more than she had paid for it. Together with her savings, it would give her enough to live on for a few months until she could find a job or otherwise decide what she wanted to do with her life.

It was the best solution to her problem of money. Although the painting was nominally Thorne's, she knew he wouldn't want it after she was gone, and she could use the money it would bring. Besides, it didn't look—right—hanging where it was, among his priceless collection. Everytime she looked at it, she was sure Thorne was secretly thinking the same thing.

The idea of selling the painting had occurred to her last night, after talking to Thorne. He had called back again after midnight, and after apologising for waking her, asked curtly, 'Where were you tonight?'

'At the movies.'

'Alone?'

'No,' she said coolly, having expected the question. 'Mrs Abernathy called and asked me to go with her. Her husband was tied up in a meeting and she was feeling restless. Afterwards, we had a pizza.'

'A meeting? I thought he was retired,' he said smoothly.

'Oh, he is, but he belongs to some of those environmental groups. This one was "Save the Whales" or something.' The lie tripped smoothly off her tongue.

He was silent, testing her words, her voice, before continuing slowly, 'I'm glad you could go. You're probably lonesome there by yourself.'

She didn't make the obvious reply. If she was leaving him tomorrow, he would understand it better if she was cool tonight.

They talked on idly, and she realised he was puzzled about her lack of enthusiasm, then as he was about to hang up, he said abruptly, 'What was the name of the movie?'

Her mind went blank. 'I'm sorry—I can't remember!' she gasped.

'I can always ask Mrs Abernathy,' he said silkily.

She drew in her breath sharply. 'Yes, why don't you do that?' she snapped and slammed down the phone.

She lay in bed, fuming. Damn him! What had she ever done to make him think she would take a lover behind his back—for that was what he had been implying! This whole hellish week had been a living nightmare and it was all his fault! He had started off by accusing her of being virtually a nymphomaniac, then she had been insulted by his old buddy, Jake, who apparently kept up a running game of girl-swapping, and then, she had to cope with his frightful ex-client who had some sort of grudge against him! Now, he was intimating that she was sleeping around—or on the verge of it! Her eyes fell on the seascape and she decided, then and there, to sell it.

Leaving the art gallery, she stopped off at the

nearest bus station to enquire about schedules to Medlar's Mill, then drove her little Skylark home and parked it in the garage for the last time. She let herself in with her key, again for the last time, reminding herself that she must remember to leave it behind. She stopped, brought up short by the sight of Thorne's suitcase standing in the middle of the hallway, as though he had dropped it as soon as he walked in the door.

Before she could take in the implications of Thorne's early return and what it would mean to her plans, he erupted from the library with all the force of a hurricane, in a white hot rage.

He glared at her ferociously. 'I wondered when you'd get home!' he snarled, and added violently, 'Get in here! I want to talk to you.'

When she hesitated, he grabbed her by the wrist and dragged her towards the library door, then slammed it behind them as soon as he had her inside.

Josey rubbed her maltreated wrist and stared at him warily. He was in the grip of a murderous rage. His face was thunderous; there was an ugly expression in his eyes, and his mouth had a hard, taut, compressed look, as though he was holding back words with an effort.

'Who in the hell was the man who you were with at dinner last night?'

She paled. 'How did you know?' she half-whispered.

A savage flare lit his eyes. 'You little slut, you didn't expect me to ever find out, did you?' His lips were barely parting to let the grating words out. 'You thought you'd covered your tracks only you forgot—there's always somebody who sees and tells: Have you slept with him yet?' When she didn't speak, he gripped her by the shoulders and shook her hard. 'I want you to answer me, so I'll know whether to kill both of you or merely beat the hell out of you! Answer me, damn you! Has he been taking care of your sexy little body this week, while I've been away?' She shook her head dazedly. 'Is he as good as I am?' he went on, oblivious to her dazed negative. His lip curled in a sneer. 'You couldn't go without it for a week, even, could you?'

'Let me go, Thorne.'

When he didn't, she repeated the words and kept repeating them until he dropped his hands. She was angry, but she was afraid to strike him for fear he would knock her down. Finally, he stepped back as though even to be near her, repelled him.

'Yes, I was with a man last night, Thorne,' she went on icily, 'and you're never going to know why or who, because I won't tell you. You may think whatever you like about it, because I won't care.' She added defiantly, 'Incidentally, this is as good a time as any to ask you for a divorce. I want one on any grounds you like, as quickly as possible.'

'Like hell! You're not walking out on me like that! You're going to stay and face the music, you cheating little bitch! I'm not letting you go until you pay me for every moment of hell you've put me through. You might even enjoy it.' He laughed harshly.

'You can't prevent me from getting a divorce,' she said steadily.

'I can go a long way towards it. I know every legal twist and turn in the book. Whatever way you turn, I'll have been there before you and slammed the door. Oh, not indefinitely, but long enough to put a crimp in your future plans. No, my dear, you're going to have to work for that divorce, and I don't think I have to tell you how.' He looked at his watch. 'I'm leaving you now—for a little while. Think over what I've said, and when I get back, I want to find you upstairs, on that bed, waiting for me.' The handsome face wore an ironical smile. 'Understand?'

'Oh, I understand, all right,' she said contemptuously. 'Go to hell.'

Something painful gleamed for a moment in the depths of his grey eyes, then he smiled mockingly, 'Gladly, my dear, so long as you accompany me.'

He slammed the door on his way out.

Now that reaction had set in, she felt ill and very cold. Wragge, coming down the hallway wiping his hands on a tea towel, looked at her anxiously.

'Are you feeling all right, Miss Josey?' he asked, then went on tentatively. 'I saw Mr Thorne was angry about something, so I thought I'd let you soothe him down first. But he—you—is everything going to be all right?'

'Yes, Wragge, everything's going to get back to normal again,' she said steadily. She forced herself to smile. 'Will you call me a cab, please?'

'A cab? B-but what about your car? Surely you're not leaving now...? Let me get you a brandy, Miss Josey...'

She ignored him by simply walking away. In her bedroom, her suitcases were where she had left them, in her closet. She picked them up and gave one final look around the room. She was leaving everything neat and tidy in the house, but her life was in a shambles. She had intended leaving Thorne a dignified note, explaining it all in detail, but she couldn't write it now. She would have to do it later, after she'd recovered from that brutal confrontation.

She was turning away when the phone rang and she picked it up. It was Tony. She had intended calling Tony from the bus station, but this was as good a time as any to tell him her decision.

'Jocelyn.' His voice was breezy and self-assured. Tony's confidence was obviously soaring. 'Glad I caught you. It's the Green Barn. You've heard of it, I'm sure. Anyway, it's on Peachtree—and I have reservations for eight o'clock. Be on time. And Jocelyn,' he added, 'you'd better make me proud of you.'

'No, Tony,' she said calmly. 'Go back and unmake your reservations and tell the buddies you've been boasting to that you're not taking Thorne Macallan's wife out tonight. I'm leaving town. I'm not letting you blackmail me.'

He drew an angry breath. 'Listen, bitch,' he snarled. 'If you don't show up tonight, I'll . . .'

'Don't threaten me!' she snapped. 'Go to the papers, if you like. Tell your story about Mrs Thorne Macallan. It won't be so important when it's known it's about his ex-wife! You see, I'm divorcing him immediately. You can't hurt him and you really can't hurt me, for I'll be far away, living under another name, when all that muck comes out.'

There was an uncertain pause, then Tony blustered, 'Now, wa-a-ait a minute, Jocelyn, baby! You're being too hasty! Maybe I was a little rough on you. A few thousand will keep me sweet. You can dig that much up, surely? Now, don't be a fool, baby. All that loot—I—we can work things out to both our advantages.'

'Shut up, Tony,' she said contemptuously. 'You make me sick. You're a snivelling, spiteful little coward and I don't want to have to listen to you ever again in this lifetime—is that clear? Do your worst to me but let me warn you—if that story does come out in the papers, I'll see to it that Stephen Vinelli hears exactly how it happened. Not only him, but your parents, too. I shall also tell him that you and his wife are having an affair.'

'Now, wait a minute, Jocelyn . . .'

She hung up, picked up her suitcases again and walked out.

'Have you called a cab, Wragge?'

'No, Miss Josey, I haven't, but . . .'

Without a word, she walked over to the phone, lifted it and spoke to the doorman downstairs in the lobby. Wragge watched her helplessly.

'Goodbye, Wragge,' she said to the old man. 'I've enjoyed knowing you. Take care of Mr Thorne.' She shook his hand formally, lifted her suitcase and walked out.

Josey's quiet departure was a vivid contrast to that of the man who had stormed out of the building ten minutes earlier. Thorne Macallan hadn't waited for the doorman to call a cab or have his car brought around—that was too passive an action. He flung himself out into the traffic and hailed one down himself, then proceeded to make the driver extremely nervous by glaring angrily at him as he gave his destination.

Thorne's odyssey had begun that morning at about six o'clock. He had checked out of his hotel room in a mad rage and paced restlessly at the airport, waiting on standby for the first available flight home. All the time, he was listening to Zoë Vinelli's taunting voice in his ear.

Women like Zoë Vinelli were nothing new to him. He had been sorry that his old friend Stephen was married to her, but even if he wasn't, Thorne would have continued to snub her many attempts to seduce him.

The bitch had known she'd got to him this morning, however. It had been in that triumphant voice of hers, and everything she said, although she'd cooed with fake sympathy at the start.

'Thorne? Zoë, here, darling. Are you awake enough to hear some bad news?'

He had been groggy but had naturally assumed something had happened to Stephen. His old friend was very worried about the takeover of his company, for all his assets were tied up in it. Zoë herself would be considerably poorer if he was unsuccessful in his attempts to ward off the bigger company's bid and although it would amuse him at the present moment to see her in that situation, he didn't want it for Stephen's sake.

The old man was good. Look at the way he'd taken that cowardly little sneak thief, Tony Leyden, back into his business after discovering him with his hand in the till. He didn't owe him a damned thing, either, but fortunately, he had listened when Thorne had suggested making Leyden sign a confession as a guarantee of good behaviour.

All of this was going through Thorne's mind as

he stared stonily at the back of the driver's head. His thoughts returned to his wife—and the other man. He was going after his name, now. They just might know it at the restaurant. Failing that, he intended to tackle Zoë again. She had claimed she didn't know him, but she had described the meeting vividly enough. The kisses they'd exchanged, Josey's hand on his arm as she whispered in his ear—Thorne's mouth tightened grimly. For a moment, his mind was sidetracked long enough to wonder what Zoë Vinelli was doing in the downtown area in an Italian restaurant. It wasn't her usual scene.

The owner of Luigi's was voluble in his fury at being left with an unpaid cheque. Thorne offered him the money but he graciously refused. No, Signor, he knew this man. He was an old customer but not a good one, understand? He was known as a notoriously bad tipper, a writer of bad cheques, a loud-mouth blustering show-off, but he, Luigi, would eventually recover his money.

Now, the girl—ah, she was something else! He kissed his fingers. According to the waitress, she had only ordered coffee, then not drank it. She had been tense and nervous, even frightened, and the waitress had overheard the man threatening her. That figured—for he was totally unworthy of her. Something shady was going on, Luigi added darkly.

Thorne left the restaurant and returned to the cab, which was waiting out front with a ticking meter. By now, his violent rage had cooled and was directed at himself. He had the man's name and he knew 'something shady' was indeed going on. He was cold with remorse and fear, but he had something to finish before he could follow his first impulse, which was to go home and straighten things out with Josey. His face was tense with impatience as he directed the driver to Stephen Vinelli's place of business, where he should find Tony Leyden at this hour of the day.

Thirty minutes later, he returned home. He met a distressed Wragge at the door and learned then that the bird had flown.

CHAPTER FOURTEEN

JOSEY spent the first night in an Atlanta hotel, where she cried a lot. The next morning, she got up and gave herself a firm lecture. She must stop weeping for lost dreams. She must start living again, without Thorne. But first, she needed a retreat—a place where she could live until she could pull the shattered pieces of her life together. She needed to go home.

As the bus neared Medlar's Mill, Josey saw that it had changed almost beyond recognition. Nothing was familiar. Seven years had put new store fronts on Main Street and new names to some of them. The pizza place where the high school gang used to hang out after school was now a car wash, and the city hall had been remodelled to look like something out of a science fiction movie.

She locked her suitcases in one of the bus station lockers, then walked towards the local real estate office. It had changed hands: there was a new name above the door. She was relieved to see that there was no-one in there she recognised, including the bright young man who took her name and specifications. She wanted a furnished place, she told him, somewhere private, even secluded. To do some writing, she added hastily, when he began to look curious.

'Writing?' He raised his eyebrows.

'I'm working on a college thesis,' she improvised hastily, off the top of her head. 'It's on the effect of a declining population on small towns.'

'Oh.' His interest waned. 'Well, this little town is not declining. There have certainly been some changes since they opened the stove factory. We're booming!' he added genially. 'Everyone's buying stoves to conserve fuel, you know. Now, from what you say, you'd prefer a house to an apartment?' Josey nodded. 'I have just the place—a small carriage house, a very pretty little place furnished with antiques.'

'What's the rent?' Josey asked hastily.

When he told her, she flinched. 'Haven't you anything cheaper?' she asked faintly.

He looked regretful. 'Not at the moment, no. I might be able to talk Mr Clark into reducing the rent some. I think he'd prefer a good tenant to a higher rent, but . . .'

'Mr Clark?'

'Heywood Clark. The carriage house is behind his home—the big house. You have to walk through his garden to reach it. I'll call him if you like.'

'I think I know him,' Josey said slowly. A thin, young face flashed before her eyes, that of a serious boy who had been in college when she was still in junior high.

'Oh?' He looked up speculatively. 'Would you rather talk to him about it?'

'No, you call him.'

He went into his office and had a short conversation on the phone, then came out smiling, a paper in his hand.

'I've written down his address for you. Go around and talk to him. He sounded agreeable to reducing the rent for you.'

Josey took the paper slowly. 'This is the old Smiley place, isn't it?'

'Yes. Heywood Clark married Ruth Smiley about five years ago, a couple of years before her parents died. That's a great old place—one of a kind.'

Josey could walk to the old Smiley place, which was only a couple of blocks off the town square, yet very private in a big, tree-filled garden surrounded by a picket fence. At the end of the driveway was a charming little cottage painted a pale, buttercup yellow. The old house itself was a big, old-fashioned place with a cupola, assorted porches and gables, and a great deal of gingerbread trim.

Heywood Clark was waiting for her on the porch, and to her surprise, he remembered her.

'Little Josey Stewart, isn't it?' he asked smilingly. 'The prettiest little girl in town.'

'It's Josey Macallan now, Heywood, but I'm getting a divorce.' She twisted the wide, gold band nervously on her finger. 'I told a stupid lie to avoid questions,' she added apologetically. 'I told the real estate man I was a student.'

'Yes, you did,' he agreed seriously. 'It wasn't true?'

'No, I just wanted to be left alone, and I didn't want to go into a lot of explanations about my divorce. I couldn't afford to keep this place long—just a month or two—until I can work out what I'm going to do.'

'You may stay as long as you like,' he said. He named a rent that was considerably less than half the original figure. 'Can you afford that?'

'Yes, but are you sure that you can?' she asked awkwardly. 'I mean—I—I wouldn't want you to lose a good tenant on my account.'

He smiled. 'Don't worry about that.'

He had been leading her towards the little house, and now they stepped up on a doll-size porch, he unlocked the front door and threw it open. Josey saw dimly a small living room with an uneven brick floor covered by a braided rug. Beyond, a faint gleam of copper indicated a kitchen. Then, Heywood drew back the curtains, revealing a cosily furnished living room with a bar dividing it from the kitchen. Most of its furniture were antiques, simple rustic pine and maple which had been softened by deep, checked cushions and big squashy pillows. There was even an old-fashioned wood stove.

'It's chilly in here right now, but I'll soon have it warm for you.' He had adjusted the thermostat and now, he knelt before the stove and touched a match to the fire. 'Go ahead and look around while I get things organised for you.'

When Josey returned from her tour of inspection, she said sincerely, 'I like your little house, Heywood. It's beautifully furnished.'

'Thank you. My wife was the interior decorator.'

'Ruth?'

He looked up uncertainly. 'You know about Ruth?'

'Yes. She did a great job on it.'

'Yes, she did, didn't she?'

It was the faint note of reserve in his voice that made Josey hesitate to say anything more about his wife, but he offered in a friendly voice to drive her to the bus station to retrieve her luggage, then stop off at the grocery store so she could buy some food. However, when they got back, after carrying in the suitcases, he handed Josey the key and left her strictly alone—for which she was thankful.

In spite of its surface neatness, Ruth had allowed the little house to get into a sad shape. The copper-bottomed pans above the stove were dull, and the furniture had a film of grey dust on it. The next morning, Josey plunged into an orgy of cleaning, polishing the brass and copper, scrubbing and waxing the brick floor, even washing the windows. She welcomed the hard work. She wanted to make herself so tired that she would have no trouble in sleeping at night.

When she rested between cleaning jobs, she played solitaire, or listened to the radio, or just sat and remembered. Those were the worst moments, when she ached to be in Thorne's arms, no matter what he might say to her. When that happened, she would leap up and plunge into some new job, or go for a walk.

She walked for miles that weekend—in town and on country roads, keeping her head down if she met anyone. Medlar's Mill was too far south to have snow, but the weather was cold and the wind sharp. The fields were rimed with frost early in the morning and the corn stubble rattled desolately in the wind.

She liked this little town she'd grown up in, but she didn't think she would want to stay on after the month or two she had given herself. She'd need a job, but she thought she'd want to return to Atlanta, where she'd be near Thorne— at least, geographically. But she didn't allow herself to dwell on it. Right now, she was living from hour to hour—tomorrow, she would start trying to make it one day at a time.

She had been in the house for three days when she met Heywood again. She was returning from one of her walks late in the afternoon, when his car pulled into the driveway. He got out, with a briefcase in his hand.

'Are you making it all right?'

'Yes, fine.' She forced a cheerful smile.

'How about a cup of coffee?'

She hesitated, then said, 'All right. I'd like to meet Ruth.'

He had been brushing his feet on the doormat but at that, his head came up sharply.

'I thought you knew. Ruth is dead.'

'Oh, no, I didn't!' Josey gasped. 'Oh, I'm so sorry! I . . . I wouldn't have said . . .'

'No, of course not. Don't worry about it.' He opened the door and led the way into the big, old-fashioned kitchen. 'She died about a year ago. She was ill for six months before that. The little house was one of the last things she did. It gave her a great deal of pleasure—planning its furnishings.'

'Yes, yes, of course.' Josey said mechanically, wretchedly conscious of her blunder and his change of mood.

However, as he got out the coffee and filled the coffee maker, he became more cheerful. He talked about his work. Josey learned that he was a consulting engineer with an office in the house, and he did a lot of travelling. He did almost none, he told her, during his wife's illness, but he was now back on the road again, most of the time. It kept him from thinking about Ruth too much and besides, the house was lonely. Everywhere he went, it reminded him of Ruth, but he didn't want to sell it because it had been her family home. And because he couldn't bear to give up this last link to Ruth.

When he said the last, Josey knew what he

meant. She would have felt the same way about Thorne. She could understand his pain: merely the thought of Thorne no longer living in the same world squeezed her heart with agony.

It had been a big decision to put the little house up for rent, because he hadn't wanted people intruding on his sorrow, but now that it had been done, he thought he would continue to rent it, he told Josey. It helped to know it was occupied.

After a while, Josey rose to go, surprised to find it was already dark outside. They had talked a long time—or rather, Heywood had—and she thought it had been good for him. He had needed this—a general purging of the spirit.

She walked slowly back to the house, thinking about him. As she pushed open the door, which she had carelessly left unlocked, she was alerted by an instinct as old as time. A faint, subtle scent assailed her nostrils—the familiar scent of Thorne's after-shave lotion mixed with leather and his favourite Scotch. Josey pressed the light switch.

'Hello, Josey,' he said calmly.

CHAPTER FIFTEEN

'WHAT are you trying to do—scare me to death? How did you get in here? Don't you know breaking and entering is against the law?'

She was talking too much, of course, but she was thrown off-balance by the sight of the tall, lean figure in the little room that had become her haven. It was so *good*—so incredibly wonderful—to have him here, whatever his reason for it was. And he was smiling at her, sitting in her favourite armchair—trust Thorne to choose the most comfortable one!—legs outstretched, a glass of Scotch comfortably balanced on his chest. When he stood up in that swift, supple movement that was particularly his own, she wanted to hug him from joy.

'If you'll slow down long enough to let me get in a word edgewise, I'll explain,' he drawled lazily, reaching for her coat. 'The door was open and I walked in. No breaking, just entering.' He walked to the tiny coat closet and hung her coat beside his own.

'Looks like you've already made yourself at home,' she said tartly, trying to bring herself down to earth. He was, after all, here to see about the divorce and it was dangerous for her to forget it.

'Why not?' He grinned. 'I had to wait somewhere and you seemed prepared to remain over there next door indefinitely. Shall I get you a Scotch?'

'No. Why didn't you turn on the light?'

He smiled grimly. 'I thought it might scare you and you'd run back and get help. It seemed wiser to keep our first meeting between ourselves.'

'Oh.' She stared at him solemnly, her eyes like two golden pools in her pale face. 'How did you find me?'

'I called Maud when I couldn't remember the name of this place. Fortunately, she had heard you mention it, and having a retentive memory was able to come up with it.'

'How is Maud?'

'Worried. Missing you. Anxious about you.'

Her head dropped. 'I didn't want to worry her.'

'I know. I only called her because I had nowhere else to turn to.'

'How did you know I'd be here?'

'You had to be somewhere, Josey, and when you weren't with Maud or the Abernathys . . .'

'You went to them?' Josey was horrified.

'I went to anyone I thought could help me find you. I got here early this morning then had to wait for that real estate place to open when the motels turned up a blank. I've wasted hours driving around, waiting for that damned officious little real estate man to leave his office. He wouldn't tell me anything but when he was out to lunch, I got one of the girls to show me his rental book.'

'I can imagine,' Josey drawled sarcastically, but her eyes were bright. She was pleased that he had wanted to see her badly enough to go to some trouble to search for her. 'You charmed her into it, naturally?'

His grin held a touch of complacency. 'A combination of that and bribery.'

She said abruptly, 'Would you like some coffee? Or—another Scotch?'

'I'd like some food,' he said frankly. 'I haven't had a bite all day. I was on the road at breakfast time and I missed lunch waiting for that real estate man to leave his office.'

'I'm afraid I just have eggs,' she said doubtfully. 'I don't keep much food in the house.'

'Eggs are fine. I like eggs,' he said gravely, following her into the kitchen.

She opened the refrigerator door. 'Oh, here's some cheese—and there's milk, of course—and bread . . .' She was chattering but she found his nearness unnerving.

He sat down on one of the bar stools and watched her steadily while she cracked eggs into a bowl and grated cheese for an omelette. All the time she worked, she was conscious of his eyes. Why was he here? About the divorce, of course, but why had he found a personal visit necessary? After the harsh words they'd exchanged, she would have thought he'd never want to see her again. She looked up and something about his watchful face made her say, 'You look like you didn't get much sleep last night?'

'I haven't got much sleep for three days. Aren't you going to eat anything?'

'I'm not hungry.'

'Am I taking all your food, Josey?' He smiled slightly.

'As a matter of fact, you are,' she said coolly. 'But I owe you a meal or two.'

She slid the omelette, bouffant and golden, on to the waiting plate, then added toast and coffee. He didn't talk while he was eating, but she saw he was enjoying his food. Finally, he pushed his plate back.

'Do you like this little house?'

She answered vaguely, 'It's very nice but the rent is rather high. Heywood reduced it for me, but of course, I wouldn't want to take advantage of his generosity for long.'

He nodded, then rose and carried his dishes to the sink where she was scrubbing the omelette pan for the third time. She looked at him nervously.

'I guess you are here about the divorce?' she blurted out the words she hadn't intended to say first. 'I was going to write to you as soon as I got a permanent address . . .'

He leaned forward and put his finger on her lips. He was smiling, his eyes glinting with that look that had the power to make her knees weak.

'Why *did* you come, Thorne?' she mumbled around his finger.

'I came to take you back with me.' When she merely stared at him, he added, 'To live with me. To be my love, my partner, my wife—all of those things we merely played at before. To make a real marriage.'

She drew a long, shuddering breath. Now that the time had come to confess, she found herself quite calm. 'That's impossible,' she said almost matter-of-factly. 'If you knew the truth about me, you'd want a divorce.'

'Josey, darling.' With gentle hands, he drew her away from the sink and into his arms, where he held her quietly. She stood stiffly, breathing in the familiar masculine odour of his skin, letting the comforting warmth of his body relax her slightly. 'There is nothing, absolutely nothing, Josey Macallan, that you could tell me about yourself that would make me want a divorce— except that you didn't love me anymore, and even then, I would still want you.'

'Don't say that,' she said brokenly. 'Please don't say that. I am—I *must* file f-for a divorce.'

'Come and tell me about it,' he said comfortably, leading her into the living room and putting her into the big armchair. He kicked the footstool beside the chair and sat down on it, his long legs folding themselves under it. He took her hand. 'Tell me.'

'I am wanted for parole violation,' she said bluntly, not looking at him.

'Why?' Just that one word, but something unsurprised about it made Josey look at him. He was watching her calmly.

'I am a felon—an ex-convict. I—was Tony Leyden's partner when he was convicted of theft. You were his defence attorney.' She kept her eyes on him desperately as the words poured out, waiting for the look of disgust, the inevitable change of expression. 'Those things you said about me in court weren't true—maybe some of them were—but I hadn't known about the money. Tony asked me to keep a box of mementoes for him. But he did spend money on me and he *did* lend me money to pay my rent,' she added painfully. 'My lawyer said it was no use—it would be much easier on me to plead guilty and let the judge suspend sentence.' His face changed to a look of raw fury and she stopped, frightened.

'Go on,' he said in a controlled voice.

'I thought you were going to defend me when you started talking to the judge. Funny, isn't it?' she asked bitterly. 'You were Tony's lawyer but I thought you were going to defend *me*!'

He was squeezing her hand so tightly that it had whitened from the pressure. His face was like a teak carving, hard, cold and implacable.

'Go on, finish it,' he muttered between set lips.

'That's why I screamed at you,' she whispered tiredly. 'I felt—betrayed.'

'You *were* betrayed.' His voice was filled with the bitterness of self-condemnation, but his eyes were naked with pain. 'By the system, by all of us. Tony, who lied, and your lawyer, who was too lazy and incompetent to represent you properly. And I was the worst of all, because I was so biased and gullible that I swallowed every one of Tony's lies without question. And the Judge, who didn't even bother to look beyond my distorted version to see you as something besides the treacherous little tramp I had portrayed—as an innocent and badly frightened young girl, who hadn't been given a chance to defend herself.'

'You sound as though you already know about me,' she whispered almost disbelievingly.

He smiled wryly. 'My dear, I've known who you really were since the week before I married you.'

Her eyes opened wide, startled. 'You mean—all that time I was going through agony, worrying about it, and you *knew*! *How could you?*'

'Egotism,' he said cynically. 'You were right— I do have it. I wanted you to trust me enough to tell me of your own accord.' His twisted smile held a hint of self-derision.

'You—you bastard!' she hissed. 'You put me through all that torment—and you knew all the time!'

'Yes. It somehow became an obsession with me. If you loved me, you'd trust me enough to tell me the truth, and if you didn't, it meant you didn't love me. It was as simple as that.' He smiled without humour, watching her with a merciless intensity that somehow frightened her.

She stilled, suddenly very wary, knowing that the reply she made would be very important. 'I didn't tell you because I thought I would lose you,' she said hesitantly.

He blinked. He hadn't expected that. 'Lose me?' He frowned.

'If you learned who I was, the woman you'd despised in court, I thought you'd throw me out. You thought I betrayed Tony, that I was greedy, covetous ... I knew you wouldn't want to be married to a woman like that.'

He stared at her blankly, transfixed with horror. 'My God,' he breathed. 'That never occurred to me. I have known the truth about you for so long, it didn't occur to me you'd still think . . .' He stopped, shaking his head dumbly. 'I've known for years that you were innocent. When you ranted about me being a bad lawyer, I was angry, of course, but later, when I learned who you were, I knew you were justified. I *was* a bad lawyer. But it didn't occur to me you would assume I still felt the same way about you.'

'You mean you wouldn't have thrown me out?' Somehow, that seemed the most important thing Josey had heard yet.

He knelt beside her chair, holding her hand to his cheek. 'My darling,' he said simply, 'I would never "throw you out". You've been the sum total of my existence almost since that first day on the beach. The way I treated you after that,' he added dryly, 'was a form of self-protection because you'd become so important to me. I can't live without you. I'm not even a whole man when I'm away from you. It's as though I've lost a vital part of my body and I walk around in pain, unable to function. I need you to live.' His face was almost unrecognisable. His pallor had reduced his tan to a muddy-yellow. His mouth was a taut grimace of pain—his eyes starkly pleading. There was a look of uncertainty about him that Josey had never seen before. He looked—almost—afraid.

Thorne *frightened*? She put out her hand tentatively and touched his cheek, and he turned his face into it and kissed her palm. It was the gesture of a penitent, and Josey had never associated repentance or even fear with Thorne before. She felt a surge of tenderness.

'Thorne?' she whispered. 'I feel the same way about you.'

He kissed her softly, his lips tender and gentle on her mouth, her eyelids, her cheeks, the edges of her lips. Her confidence was returning, and she ran her hands daringly inside his shirt.

'No.' He put her from him firmly. 'If, by some miracle, you're prepared to forgive me, I want to get the explanations over with now.'

'You don't have to explain anything,' she said demurely.

'Yes, I do. Josey, I've known since a few months after you were released from prison that you were innocent. Tony told me,' he added in answer to her puzzled look. 'He was working for Stephen Vinelli, and he opened his safe and stole some money. In his confession, which Stephen and I had him write and sign, he admitted that he framed you that other time. Stephen and I were appalled at what we'd done to you and I tried to find you through your parole officer so we could make amends.' His glance at her was questioning.

Haltingly, she explained what had happened and watched his face set ominously. 'I see.' Grimly, he added, 'I went after your lawyer then, and gave the fool a lesson in law he'll never forget. Josey,' he added swiftly, 'you were cleared of all charges on the court books five years ago. In the eyes of the law, you're innocent.'

So it had all been for nothing! The running; the changing of her name; the five years with John when she'd literally hidden from the world behind closed doors—it had all been unnecessary! But somehow, that fact—the wasted years—weren't so important as that it had been Thorne who had done it, who had realised his mistake and made retribution; then waited patiently for an opportunity to tell her.

'I didn't know,' she whispered. Her face was wet with tears and he lifted a long, lean finger and wiped them away from her cheeks.

'How could you?' he asked slowly. 'I was afraid to tell you because I knew you had good reason to hate me.'

'No, not hate.' She smiled shakily. 'We were both fools. I thought I married you for revenge then realised on our honeymoon that I loved you.'

He drew a deep breath, his eyes blazing with leaping lights. There was a suppressed note of exultation in his voice as he replied, 'Neither of us could understand our emotions. I couldn't be around you for five minutes without going into a tailspin—you had me coming and going. I started out by hating you and wanting to make love to you at the same time.' He grinned faintly. 'I told myself it would be easy when you responded so positively—but I was by no means as confident of my technique as I pretended. I wasn't even sure if you really disliked me or were merely being provocative.'

'And then you went away, leaving me to mend my shattered defences with Brian's help.'

He grimaced. 'That—*puppy*! Do you have any idea what you did to me when you said he'd had you that night I waited up late? I nearly went insane! My sweet innocent, don't you recognise raw sexual jealousy when you see it?' He laughed harshly. 'God knows, I've demonstrated enough of it since we've been married! I was so utterly unsure of you. The night I stormed in on your date, I'd just learned who you were and I was desperate. I knew you despised me. The best I could hope for was to get you into my bed, then perhaps I could make you fall in love with me— eventually. When you mentioned marriage, I sat there stunned, unable to believe my luck, searching for flaws in your words. I knew you didn't love me but I thought if I could keep you wanting me, our marriage had a chance.'

She flushed. 'I did try to back out,' she muttered defensively.

'That you did! But I wouldn't let you, would I?' He laughed joyously.

'You thought I married you for your money, didn't you?'

'Not exactly money—I knew you better than that by then. But the things I could give you, the lifestyle, all of that, yes. It was better than believing you hated me so much, you married me for revenge. So I used it all—money, sex—to keep you, until you levelled with me. You had to be the one to tell me—I wouldn't settle for anything less. So I kept on testing you, picking quarrels, making love . . . God, at times the only thing that kept me sane was your sexual response! Yet I hated that, too, when I thought that was all you wanted from me.'

Josey could understand that. She had felt the same way. 'How did you learn who I was?'

'I put my staff on it when I returned to Atlanta with Eve. When they hadn't made any progress by the time I finished with the court case in Charleston, I returned and went through the files myself.' He smiled slightly. 'When the computer threw up Tony Leyden's name, I remembered.' He looked at her painfully. 'My darling, if I live to be a hundred—a thousand!—I'll never make it up to you for what I did.'

'No, Thorne—it wasn't altogether your fault . . .'

'No excuses!' He said harshly. 'I was blindly prejudiced. I thought I knew people—what made them tick—their motivations. I knew nothing!' He added remotely, 'When I realised what I had done to you, I joined my father's firm, which specialises in civil cases, big business accounts— that sort of thing. I no longer felt competent to defend cases in criminal court.'

'Thorne!' Josey was appalled. 'It wasn't all your fault! Your mother—a-and f-father . . .!'

The pale grey eyes warmed at her stammered words of sympathy. 'Yes, Josey, my parents may have contributed, but I did it to myself, my darling. And I didn't learn my lesson. I did it a second time when I jumped to conclusions about your place in Maud's life. I need you in my life, my dearest heart,' he added thickly. 'I need you for my eyes and ears—to help me see people as they really are. To help me when my cynicism threatens to blind my viewpoint.'

'Like Elaine and Ralph.' She smiled at him teasingly.

'Yes, even Ralph,' he agreed drily. 'Irritating but harmless—and certainly not to be taken seriously. Yet I made that evening miserable for you with my jealousy.'

'Zoë Vinelli did her share,' she said drily, then remembered. Her cheeks whitened. 'Thorne, I'd forgotten! Tony . . .'

'Are you speaking of his threats to take your story to the scandal sheets?' he asked her calmly, pulling her into his arms.

She started. 'You know?'

'I know,' he said gravely. 'And have successfully spiked his sordid little blackmail plot—with Stephen's help.'

'How?' she asked fearfully.

'With the written confession he signed after robbing Stephen. It can earn him a second prison term if we care to pursue it. And this time, he'll get no leniency. I assure you,' he added, with a narrowed smile. 'Tony saw the light after it had been pointed out to him. Stephen is in no mood to compromise this time—especially when he learned that Tony and his wife were having an affair. It was her jealousy of you that prompted her to make trouble by informing me. Of course, she never dreamed Tony would get caught in the backlash.'

'But she must know about me!' Josey licked dry lips. 'And she'll tell Eve Sanders and . . .'

'No.' His face flared with a raw anger that threatened retribution for Zoë. 'She won't talk. Not if she knows what's good for her. Her life of luxury depends on Stephen's continued generosity, and he has had his eyes opened. However, just to nullify your fears, I suggest we start telling our friends about your prison experience and the villainous part I played in it. As a romance, it will make the cocktail circuit. We'll probably be able to dine out on it for some time.' His mouth quirked. 'Haven't you learned from Maud that the more outrageous a story is, the more acceptable it becomes? We're sure to be a nine-days' wonder, then something will come along to take our place.'

He slipped in beside her and pulled her into his lap. 'Stop worrying, my beauty, we're over the worst. From now on, everything's going to be coming up roses.' For long moments they rested there, arms tightly around each other. Josey felt at peace for the first time since that fateful Sunday afternoon when the police brought her the news of her parents' death. He rested his head against her bright hair, and she felt a deep thankfulness that she had come full circle to this point. Oh, there would be more bumps in the future—braving the curious eyes would be one—but with Thorne beside her, she couldn't count them as any more substantial than air puffs in the wind.

'Do you think you'll ever forgive me for what I did to you?' Thorne's voice was muffled against her hair.

She looked up, shocked that he could still be wondering about that. 'Darling, I forgot it long ago! Besides, if it hadn't happened the way it did, we wouldn't have met and be here now, like this.'

He smiled slightly, but his eyes were shadowed. 'I don't deserve that you should forgive me, but I thank God for your generosity. I love you, Josey, and I will never knowingly make you unhappy again. I'll make it up to you, I promise you that.'

'Don't try to spoil me!' she scolded. 'I'll become impossible—and you've already called me a shrew!'

He smiled. 'Very well, I won't spoil you if you'll love me.' He rose with her in his arms and started striding towards the bedroom.

'You act like a man who knows just where he's going,' she commented blandly.

'I told you I was alone here for at least two hours. Plenty of time to discover the bed and establish squatters' rights. I was determined I was staying the night—either in the bed with you or out there in that armchair.'

His suitcase was laying open on the bed and he swept it off then ripped back the patchwork coverlet and blankets, all in one swift movement. Then, he turned to her.

But she was already removing his shirt, her hands sliding smoothly over the hardening muscles of his shoulders. Her eyes were shining with a demure mischief that delighted him. The discovery of his love had restored her self-confidence and shown her in a new light—as the kind of woman she should be, one who was aware of her powers because she knew she was loved. For a long moment, he watched her, his eyes observing the smiling eyes; the dimple playing at the corner of her lips; the faint hint of fugitive colour on her cheekbones as she unbuckled his belt. He placed his trembling hand over her fingers.

'Let me,' he said huskily, stripping off his remaining clothes.

He undressed her slowly, savouring every moment as his eyes roamed hungrily over her slim, taut body. By this time, they were both breathing heavily and when he picked her up, she clung to his neck, planting quick warm kisses on his throat and the broad expanse of his shoulders. From beneath heavy-lidded eyes, she could see that his face had become a rigid mask of desire.

He placed her on the bed, his long, lean length following. She could feel his muscles hardening against the soft flesh of her belly. Unwilling to wait, she pulled him fiercely into her body, her desire a raging, primitive force of its own, spiralling her higher and higher towards the peaks of rapture. At its very height, he proclaimed his love for her over and over in a husky murmur, and she was sure heaven could promise no greater glory.

Much later, lying in his arms, she said prosaically, 'I'm hungry.'

He burst out laughing. 'Is there an all-night hamburger stand in town?'

'Probably, but I think I can find some soup.' As she started to rise, his grip tightened and she looked back into his kindling eyes. She sank back slowly. 'On the other hand, I can eat soup anytime. We have all night for soup.'

Here's how to get this special offer from Harlequin! As simple as 1…2…3!

AUGUST
TREASURY EDITION
COUPON

1. Each month, save one Treasury Edition coupon from your favorite Romance or Presents novel.
2. In four months you'll have saved four Treasury Edition coupons (<u>only one coupon per month allowed</u>).
3. Then all you have to do is fill out and return the order form provided, along with the four Treasury Edition coupons required and $1.00 for postage and handling.

Mail to: Harlequin Reader Service

RT1-A-2

In the U.S.A.
P.O. Box 52040
Phoenix, AZ 85072-2040

In Canada
P.O. Box 2800, Postal Station A
5170 Yonge Street
Willowdale, Ont. M2N 6J3

Please send me my FREE copy of the Janet Dailey Treasury Edition. I have enclosed the four Treasury Edition coupons required and $1.00 for postage and handling along with this order form.

(Please Print)

NAME_____

ADDRESS_____

CITY_____

STATE/PROV._____ ZIP/POSTAL CODE_____

SIGNATURE_____
This offer is limited to one order per household.

This special Janet Dailey offer expires January 1986.

SUPPLIES LIMITED

You're invited to accept 4 books and a surprise gift **Free!**

Acceptance Card

Mail to: Harlequin Reader Service®

In the U.S.
2504 West Southern Ave.
Tempe, AZ 85282

In Canada
P.O. Box 2800, Postal Station A
5170 Yonge Street
Willowdale, Ontario M2N 6J3

YES! Please send me 4 free Harlequin Presents® novels and my free surprise gift. Then send me 8 brand new novels every month as they come off the presses. Bill me at the low price of $1.75 each ($1.95 in Canada)—an 11% saving off the retail price. There are no shipping, handling or other hidden costs. There is no minimum number of books I must purchase. I can always return a shipment and cancel at any time. Even if I never buy another book from Harlequin, the 4 free novels and the surprise gift are mine to keep forever.

108 BPP-BPGE

Name	(PLEASE PRINT)

Address	Apt. No.

City	State/Prov.	Zip/Postal Code

This offer is limited to one order per household and not valid to present subscribers. Price is subject to change. ACP-SUB-1